DAYS

ARE

LIKE

GRASS

First edition published in New Zealand
by Eunoia Publishing Limited (NZ) 2016

For more information about our titles go to
www.eunoiapublishing.com

Text Copyright © 2016 by Sue Younger

The moral right of the author has been asserted

Cover images: running legs by Chris Coad; grassy verge by
Christopher Wesser; pounamu carved by Anthony Jenner

Design and layout by Katy Yiakmis

All characters and events in this publication, other than those clearly in the public domain, are fictitious and any resemblance to real persons, living or dead, is purely coincidental.

ALL RIGHTS RESERVED. This book contains material protected under International, New Zealand, and United States Federal Copyright Laws and Treaties. Any unauthorised reprint or use of this material is prohibited. No part of this book may be reproduced or transmitted in any form or by any means, electronic or mechanical, including photocopying, recording, or by any information storage and retrieval system without express written permission from the author/publisher. For permission requests, write to the publisher at the address below.

ISBN 978-0-9941047-6-2

Eunoia Publishing Limited
PO Box 33890, Takapuna
Auckland 0740
New Zealand

Level 13, WHK Tower
51-53 Shortland St
Auckland 1140
New Zealand

www.eunoiapublishing.com

Printed in China by Asia Pacific Offset Limited

2 4 6 8 10 9 7 5 3 1

DAYS ARE LIKE GRASS

A NOVEL

BY SUE YOUNGER

EUNOIA
PUBLISHING

"Childhood decides."
JEAN-PAUL SARTRE

"The only professionals of any use now are doctors and firemen."
MARTHA ARGERICH, CONCERT PIANIST, AFTER 9/11

1

LONDON 2009

"You remember your promise?"

"Promise?"

"Yossi, I'm moving to the other end of the earth, with my precious daughter, to a place I hate, so I can be with you. You need to promise this for me."

"Ok, Claire-Bear."

"My family is off limits. It's all I ask. You promise?"

"I promise."

"Cross your heart and hope to die?"

"What does that mean?"

2

NEW ZEALAND 1970

You don't know why you pick the girl up.

You don't even know why you're there, just south of the Bombay Hills. Maybe you'll head to your mother's in Hamilton. Ask for help. Maybe not. You can't decide. Driving, just driving, through lush green land scarred by straggly barbed-wire fencing. Trying to drive the draining voice of your wife out of your head. You should be on your way to work. But the other woman, the sweet, compliant one, is there, eye blackened by her husband, looking to you for answers. That woman worships you.

And now this girl shines in the distance. She looks like Raquel Welch, hair teased and pushed high on her head with some kind of band. She's walking along the hot, raw road, wiggling her hips like a film star, sticking out her thumb. Looks like a mirage. They're running wild, these young girls. You wouldn't want your baby daughter hitchhiking like this when she's older. You better give this one a ride, or some crazy bastard might.

She gets in the Kingswood. You offer her some beer from the crate you'd stashed in the back of the car to hide it from your wife. Her painted eyes are bewitching and she flirts like crazy while you're driving. Grabbing your arm when you make a joke, holding your hand while you light her cigarette, even brushing her arm across your groin on purpose when she reaches for your bottle of beer. She swears a lot. You've never known a woman behave like this. She wants a ride all the way to Taumarunui. You should be turning around, getting back to Auckland. She wiggles over to sit hard up against you on the big bench seat and you drink and she laughs and the miles of fertile country flash past and she flirts and you drink some more.

When you can no longer stand it you turn down a side road but she doesn't say anything. You stop. You'll have to let her out and drive back to your life. There's a paddock full of that lush, green shag-pile grass beside you and you see a mean-looking bull so you point out the beast and she laughs and squeals. You kiss her. She responds at first, like no woman you've known before. You kiss the downy skin behind her ear that's been torturing you since Pokeno and you cup your hand around the tiniest point of the sweep of her waist. She goes a bit stiff and still. But you're really turned on and you've had a lot of beer so you go a bit harder, coaxing her, telling her she's lovely and then all of sudden she's screaming and fighting. You grab her arm to calm her down and you tell her that you won't hurt her and you mean it, you would never hurt her, but she wrestles it away and she's opening the car door and climbing out. Then she's walking away in her red dress down the tar-sealed road in the heat. She's swaying and stumbling, running from you. Then she stops in the road and looks back at you, to see what you're going to do next. And that's it. Just like that. Your life, ruined.

3

STARSHIP CHILDREN'S HOSPITAL, AUCKLAND

JANUARY 2010

A FEW HOURS AFTER Yossi asks her to marry him, Claire hurries to theatre for an acute trauma case, a three-year-old hurt in a road accident. A man, obviously the father, stares at her as she walks through the bright aqua corridor. He's slumped against a doorway, horror in every muscle, rubbing his eyes, his daughter's blood on his shirt. The accident's his fault, she can tell straight away. But she can't talk to him now. She leaves him to the garish cutouts of Mickey Mouse.

She slices the wee blonde girl from nipple to navel and it's messy and bloody and slippery. Surgery takes absolute concentration. Observation, logic and experience. That's all she has at a time like this. There is a lot of bleeding in the tiny abdomen and Claire is soon blood-spattered. Every body is the same but every body is different. Claire had been amazed to realise, early on in medicine, that each person's internal organs are as individual as their faces.

Children as young as this take real dexterity. Skinny baby birds, no room to move. Even working out what is what inside a belly is an art. Never share that with parents though; they're sure it's pure science.

Claire pokes her fingers deeper, locating the bowel, looking for the source of the bleeding, trying not to think about the father outside. Unravelling, no doubt. He hasn't had a chance to ask anything, understand anything. She'll talk to him as soon as she's finished.

"It was Dad's first access visit since the separation," says one of the nurses.

"Oh God," says another.

"Quiet please," Claire says. Running her fingers along the bloody loops, she thinks she finds something. Leaning right in to see the delicate meat in her hands her cheek is almost brushing the skin on the child's belly. There it is, another tear. She shows it to her registrar and nods to him to start stitching.

After her shower, there's a phone-call from Yossi. He and Roimata will head over to Waiheke Island straight after school. It's going to be a beautiful evening and he's bought salmon.

"Claire, I am so happy. Do you feel happy?"

"Well, Yossi, I do – I have to go. They're waiting for me upstairs."

Up on the ward, she discharges little Eli Tipene. Checking the fine red line of scar where she has operated on his diaphragmatic hernia, she admires her own neat stitching.

"He's doing so well," she tells the baby's shy fifteen-year-old mother. "Babies heal fast. Try to relax and treat him normally now. You're doing a great job."

Before she hands him back she gives him a cuddle, his fat baby smell delicious, his rabbit's ear skin soft on her cheek. So robust, so chuckly. Only last week she'd been fishing his organs out of his chest cavity and stitching them where they belonged, repairing the hole that allowed them to grow through into the wrong place and crowd his lungs. Four hours of risky surgery.

There's no father in evidence. The mother's fifteen. The same age as her Roimata. She's texting away the whole time Claire is talking to her. Still, a bright bumblebee mobile buzzes over his cot and photos of whānau smile down at him, many of whom have visited mum and baby. Her family and friends have been polite to staff, tender towards the baby and warm to the other patients on the ward. This is more than she can say for many of her patients.

This baby was seriously at risk at birth. Now that she has done her work with the scalpel, it is the love he gets that will determine his outcome.

"Where's your aunty?" she asks the girl.

"Gone to get the car."

"Sorry I missed her."

The girl's elegant and beautifully spoken aunt has been a strong and sensible presence on the ward. She's been there every day. But as Claire goes to get in the lift, the doors open and she almost bumps into Rachel Rakena, carrying a car seat. Claire smiles at her, pleased she will get to say goodbye after all.

"I've just discharged Eli. You're free to go now."

"Ah, Doctor." The woman's cheeks are red, and there's a deep frown line on her forehead. "Are you in a hurry now?"

"I'm just doing rounds and then I have surgery."

"I need to talk to you about something." She looks around her to see if anyone is listening. "I've just left a card in your office."

Claire, who's been impressed with this woman's calm demeanour throughout Eli's illness and surgery, moves closer to her, looking hard at her.

"Well, sorry, I only have a minute or two now. But I could talk to you later."

Eli's mum pokes her head out of his room. "We're all ready to go, Aunty. He's a bit grizzly, so shall I feed him before we go?"

Rachel continues to look at Claire.

"No, we'll go now. Thank you Doctor. You've been marvellous. I don't want to take up your time. I've written about it in the card."

With that she reaches for Claire and kisses her on each cheek. The car seat bangs against Claire's leg. But the woman holds her, staring at her face, her eyes searching Claire's. Then someone else gets in the lift and Claire can't hold it up any more.

"Bye then. Bye beautiful –" she singsongs, waving to the baby as the lift doors close. Rachel is still staring at her, frowning with concentration, not moving.

What was that about? She could be nervous about taking Eli

home, but it seems more personal. Claire becomes conscious of her tight breathing and a slight tingle in her hands. It seemed to be important. Please don't let it be about Claire's father.

The next patient is on the bright pink ward a floor below.

"Hi sweetheart, I hear you've got a grumbly appendix. How old are you?"

"Thikth," says the girl, lisping.

"Thikth. Wow!" Claire and the parents giggle. "You don't need your silly appendix. We'll take it out and your tummy will feel much better."

The girl holds out her doll, pointing to the scar drawn on its tummy. The Play Therapists have been, then. In the past, parents comforted their own children in hospital, explained things to them. She wonders whether the evidence is there for play therapy.

"I'm Claire Bowerman. I'm the surgeon who'll be operating," she says to the girl's exhausted parents, wondering whether they, too, are noticing her surname. She could change it when she marries Yossi. Then people like Rachel Rakena will never connect her with her notorious father. She tries to imagine introducing herself to this family as 'Dr Shalev'. Too weird. Getting married was something she never thought she'd do, let alone taking her husband's name. Maybe she'll just make up a surname.

"You're pretty. You look like a princess," the girl says.

Claire blushes.

"Thank you, darling. You look like a princess too."

The parents both laugh and Dad, holding his daughter on his knee, cuddles in tight.

It must be acute appendicitis day. Three appendectomies and a tricky bowel reconstruction later Claire stretches and flexes her shoulders, realises it's mid-afternoon. The lunch that Yossi made her is still sitting in the fridge in the staff room. The Charge Nurse on the surgical ward is there, hiding from a demanding young nursing student. In the last two months Claire's watched Janet deal with devastated families, egotistical surgeons, a dangerous scarcity of resources and rampant political correctness with aplomb, humility, and a cheerful common sense that can't be taught. She's small, and she smiles a lot, but people tend to do what she says. She's married to Sam, and the two are Claire's closest allies amongst the mostly older, male doctors at the hospital.

Janet's been the one and only person to mention Claire's father to her since she's been back. "Your father was Patrick Bowerman, right? I remember because my family vaguely knew Kathryn Phillips' family. What happened to him?"

"We don't really keep in touch."

"Fair enough."

Some people can get away with this sort of directness. At least the air was clear.

She sits down at the table next to Janet and unwraps the panini Yossi has filled with salad and cheese for her. He's so kind, and looks after her so well.

"Janet, Eli Tipene's aunt asked me some questions this morning about my family. Do you think people notice? Do they connect me with my father?"

Janet looks up from her newspaper.

"Only one person has asked me about you. One of the nurses."

A longing for the anonymity of London rises in her throat. It's physical, like a craving. She's agreed to a year here, though Yossi wants to settle forever. It's going to be a lot easier if she swallows her feminist principles and changes her name to Shalev.

She puts down the panini, her hunger gone.

What will she do about Roimata's name? Roimata has always been Bowerman, like Claire. As Yossi's been a father to her since she was five, perhaps she will want to become Shalev too, so that they can all share a name? It's actually a nice thought.

A medical student is waiting in her office to ask advice about a patient. While she listens to the young woman, Claire tears open a card that is sitting on her desk. A photo and a letter fall out.

The student is hesitant and indecisive as Claire questions her.

"You can't leave it to others all the time. You may as well not be there if you're going to do that."

Now she's been too harsh. The girl looks tearful.

"I'm sorry. I'm a bit stressed today. More of the same for twenty-four hours as you suggest. You're doing fine. And it's definitely better to doubt yourself than to think you know everything. Don't hesitate to come to me if you are worried."

The girl gone, Claire can look at the photo. It's a black and white studio shot, the white edging faded to yellow. The Māori woman is about twenty, dressed in wartime padded shoulders, her eyebrows thin crescents, her lips painted and full. The soft focus, pin-up girl look that makes everybody's Nana look beautiful in photos.

Dear Dr. Bowerman,
Thank you again for the excellent care you took of my great-nephew Eli Tipene. Your compassion and skill has been a godsend to us through this difficult time.
But it is something else I am writing to you about. When I was in your office, the name Roimata on a child's drawing caught my eye. It is not a name I expect to see in a pākehā doctor's office. Then I saw the photo of your daughter and the likeness to my grandmother made me catch my breath.

That's what it is. The resemblance to Roimata is startling. Gazing at the camera, thick black hair curling to her shoulders, she looks stern, as Roi often looks in photos. That confident warmth that resides somewhere in the tilt of the head, the arch of the eyebrows, the broad straight shoulders. It's Roimata.

I am enclosing a picture of her, Roimata Te Hira. She was an amazing woman. She brought me up. She died ten years ago and we all miss her very much. You will see the resemblance.
I thought her name an extraordinary coincidence.

I know this might be a painful and difficult matter. I'm going to be in Auckland in a few days, when I have settled my niece and Eli here. I will call you.

Nā mihi,
Rachel Rakena

She has little visual memory of him, other than powerful arms, masses of curly hair, soft skin. She remembers entering the war graveyard on the banks of the Arno, with its bright lawns and rows and rows of white headstones, hearing the hymn *Whakaaria Mai* floating through the warm sunshine to her from the New Zealand section. She'd thought she must be imagining things, shivered at the sound of this song that could only mean home. But she'd followed the sound and there he'd been, singing and weeping, one hand touching his grandfather's white stone.

She'd pretended not to be listening, busied herself reading graves near by. As his song finished the cicadas seemed to quieten too. She'd raised her head when she'd felt him looking at her and he had smiled and beckoned her over.

There had been deep sadness as they'd wandered through the graves talking. She was twenty-six and most of these men had not lived that long. All those New Zealanders buried so far from home.

Their simple lunch in the warm open air nearby, his funny stories and easy laugh. The way he'd looked down at her in the middle of the night in her cramped *pensione* and told her she was beautiful but that he couldn't spend the whole night, couldn't see her any more and him walking out the door.

She'd told no-one and had thought no-one would ever know. Bloody small world, bloody New Zealand.

Te Hira was the name all right. Brent. She'd never imagined this would happen.

Up on her office wall, the traitorous framed picture of an exuberant sunflower tilts crookedly, ROIMATA in neat teacher's handwriting marching across the top right hand corner of the paper. In a moment of sentiment, she'd called her Roimata after the grandmother the man had talked about so fondly. A way of giving her baby one small piece of him, somehow.

Next to the sunflower hangs a recent photo of Roi, playing her violin, her face rapt in concentration and beside her, one of

Yossi, standing outside Blue Bike, his Camden record shop, in winklepickers and a pea coat.

Claire sits with her head in her hands for a long time.

4

BY THE TIME SHE GETS down to the ferry she's exhausted. It's warm enough to sit upstairs on the deck. Seagulls hover and wheel, their screeches loud even above the noisy motor. The wharves shrink and disappear. Claire looks at the skyline, trying to remember what it looked like when she was young, with no Sky Tower, no skyscrapers. Even now the city looks small with the Hauraki Gulf licking at its rim.

Her hand fiddles with the letter in her pocket. From time to time she pulls out the photo and looks at it. Most people are down in the carpeted cabin, sipping wine or beer. Laughter drifts up. It's Friday night so the ferry is full of weekenders, looking forward to two days of sun and wine tasting.

Yossi picks her up at Matiatia in their little dinghy. He's brown and barefoot, his long hair is messy, and stubble flecks his chin. His smile still makes her heart lurch. So warm. So smart.

"Isn't it gorgeous? Sorry I had to stay so late at work." She climbs into the boat.

"It's going to be a busy weekend," he says, pointing at the lines of four-wheel drives meeting the ferry. The rich have moved onto Waiheke Island while Claire has been away, planting vineyards and olive groves. There are cafes and gift shops now. She left it a real frontier-land with makeshift baches, the odd hippy commune, and a raft of sickness beneficiaries living cheaply. Never mind, at least there's good coffee and good food on the island now.

As they leave the chaos of the wharf behind, Claire catches Yossi's eye and laughs out loud about the way he's looking at her.

"I know you want to know about the wedding," she says, "I want to marry you, I do. It's just, well, I'm keen to go back to London in a year and you want to stay here."

"I thought of a date. Saturday April the 17th. That gives us a couple of months. It should still be warm. Let's do it here. Maybe on the jetty."

She'd assumed it would be a quick trip to the Registry Office.

"I think we can feed everybody at the bach," Yossi says.

"Everybody?" Claire laughs. "Where is this cast of thousands coming from?"

"Ha. You're right. There's Debs, of course, and Charlotte. You might want to ask Sam and Janet. I might ask Arie, that Israeli guy I told you about who works at Marbecks Records."

He's not listening to her. She wants to go back to London. She'd only agreed to a year.

Yossi's still cautious in the boat. He steers well away from the rocks, even though the water's flat and calm tonight. They round the point and there's Ruby Bay. It's on the unfashionable side, reachable only by boat or a half hour walk through bush. Still just the six baches, all along the one track up from an old jetty. These days, on summer weekends, the bay is full of millions of dollars worth of boats.

No-one used the bach while Claire was in London. Her mother inherited it from her family but never liked Waiheke. When Claire fled Auckland after medical school, she'd put the house to the back of her mind where it had sat empty and undisturbed, the rates paid from her mother's estate.

Every weekend this summer she and Yossi have laboured, knocking down walls, opening the bach up to light and sunshine, lifting lino, sanding and polishing floorboards, painting. It's brought them closer than ever, having a project together like this. She's not yet convinced it was worth it, though, coming back to this country with such bad memories for her. She's done it for Yossi; he wanted it so much. His judgment is often better than hers. She wants him to be happy. Scary, that she's allowed love to make her so vulnerable.

Tonight there are five enormous luxury boats moored away from the jetty, tied together. Yossi gives a low whistle.

"Unbelievable," he says.

All the toys are there: jet skis, kayaks, windsurfers. Claire hopes there won't be a party tonight.

Claire and Yossi enjoy the influx of boats, though. The happy voices drifting across the water, the winking lights on the masts at nights, the constant movement in and out of the bay.

The air is thick around them. People are still swimming and the smell of fish cooking comes from the bigger boats. There it is, the blue corner of the house peeping at her through the huge pohutukawa tree. The rundown jetty. The deserted pebbly beach with the four or five rowboats that have always been there, paint peeling, solid wood, many homemade. Peace and sanctuary. There is something about ageing that makes her find a deep love for this bush, this sea, the plants and birds and the vast skies of her childhood. Weird. As if she cared about landscape when she was young. She was always studying, eyes on the prize. Study, qualify, and leave. As long as she can remember, that was her agenda.

Yossi ties up and jumps onto the jetty, barefoot and nimble. He holds out a thin hand to help her. Debs, in togs and a bright red and white sarong, comes down the track to help them carry stuff. Getting to know their neighbour at Ruby Bay has been an unexpected pleasure of returning. She's like a favourite sofa, comfy, unpretentious, solid.

When Debs had introduced herself while Claire was sunbathing and reminded her that they used to play together at Ruby Bay as kids, Claire had been a bit dismayed. Only her fourth day here and already someone recognized her. Typical. Then Yossi had come along and invited Debs over for a drink.

"Claire you poor thing," Debs is saying now. "You must be exhausted. You're an absolute hero you know. I've poured you a wine. I've got a better idea. Let's set you up with an IV wine drip."

Like them, Debs comes to Ruby Bay almost every weekend. Even better, her 14-year-old, Charlotte, goes to the same school as Roimata and they have become firm friends. As Claire walks onto the deck of the bach, Debs hands her a drink.

"Sit down. What a long day. I put your salmon on when I saw you come into the bay."

It's a beautiful night. Cicadas clatter and hiss and serene water laps against rocks below the house. Yossi has citronella candles burning against the mosquitoes. It's getting dark now and the lights of Auckland are coming on in the distance. Claire realises she's hardly eaten all day and the salmon and salad taste delicious. She tries not to eat too fast.

"This is so good. Thank you both. Are the girls up at your bach, Debs?"

"Yep – watching stuff on their laptops."

Yossi tells Debs the news about their wedding.

"You're the first person invited," he says.

"I'm honoured. That's so exciting. Congratulations."

She gets up and hugs them in their chairs. Claire remembers Debs' recent separation and feels a pang for her friend. But if Debs is thinking about it, she's not showing any sign.

"Can I do the flowers? I think you should carry dahlias. Big, showy ones."

Yossi and Debs discuss the wedding. They make Claire dizzy with all the decisions she'll have to make. Who will marry them? Will they have a best man, bridesmaids?

Claire holds up her hands.

"Slow down, slow down. No-friends, grumpy, forty-year-old Kiwi atheist marries secular Jew. Attended by their fifteen-year-old and one neighbour. Let's not get carried away with romance and wedding-y things. A party, yes. We'll write our own vows later. I'm too tired now. Not vows, actually, more like statements of intention."

Yossi and Debs laugh.

"I'm going to promise to love you forever. It's simple," Yossi says, flinging his arms around her from behind her chair and nearly knocking her dinner off her lap.

When she's finished eating, Claire goes into the kitchen to clear up. She needs to think about Rachel Rakena. Rinsing her dishes, Claire sees her own slender reflection in the window, floating against the dense whorls of bush outside, her thick blonde hair lit by the naked bulb in the kitchen. Is she denying Roimata something? Probably. She can't lie to herself. For Claire, life comes back to survival. All she needs is to rescue herself, Roimata and Yossi. They will be fine as long as the rest of the world leaves them alone. But as Roimata gets older that gets harder. How can she deny her the chance to meet her father? She can't. She wipes the sink, rinses out the dishcloth, and grabs the bottle of wine from the fridge to take out to the deck.

5
YOSSI

After Claire leaves for work on the Monday morning, Yossi sits at the wooden table in his study with the sun on his back, reading The Times on his iPad. Martha Argerich, his favourite pianist, has cancelled yet another concert. You have to love that diva behaviour. But even daydreaming about his tempestuous Argentinian idol doesn't stop him thinking about Claire. How lost she seems, how diffident about everything. She's always prickly, but she seems brittle since they have been here.

Was he wrong to push her so hard to come back? In Camden she'd hung a photo of Ruby Bay on their lounge wall. Almost all the art she owned was figurative work by New Zealand artists: men in black singlets, sturdy, plain women, anthropomorphic birds. Some part of her must want to return, he'd been sure, in spite of her protests.

She'll be fine once she settles. She always copes, always knows what to do. She fills every moment. Even when he met her, although she'd already been in London a few years, she'd still been like a new young traveller, grabbing all the opportunities offered: the National Theatre, lectures at the Royal Society, concerts at St Martin-in-the-Fields and the Wigmore, exhibitions at the Saatchi gallery. Even if she does tease him that Martha plays too fast and is a drama queen, normally her taste is perfect. All the time working long hours and being a wonderful mother to Roimata. He envies her drive.

Not here, though. She seems tired and sad.

He tries to imagine what it's been like for her, coming home. To him, it's about safety. New Zealand is the most peaceful place on earth. There's even a popular song about it in Israel. He hums it now while he tidies up the kitchen … *to live on a green island in a distant ocean … without wars or forced loans to pay for tanks or guns …*

He makes himself a flat white with the curvaceous La Pavoni. So pleased he brought it with him. The rich smell suffuses the kitchen and stimulates his nerves. He should get on with his writing.

Bright sun bounces off the stainless steel bench. A branch shakes outside the open window. Yossi moves over slowly and is rewarded by seeing a tūī, swinging upside down on a branch, neck stretched up pecking energetically, the pristine white feathers on its throat shivering against its metallic green chest.

He's overawed by the landscape here. Vast, impenetrable ranges of hills. Bush, sea, birds, space. No corruption, not much violence. Admittedly, he finds it hard to find a decent conversation. You can sit down and talk to a New Zealander for two hours and still not have really talked about anything at all. They're so moderate. Fair and simple and generous. Middle of the road.

Claire will come around. He'll make her.

He takes his coffee to his desk. Savours its delicious bitterness and the fact he can enjoy it without rushing. But he must get on with this article. He started it years ago. It's about the concert in Israel where his parents had first met. The editor of *Granta*, a fellow music fanatic who often came into the shop, says he would be interested in publishing it. Claire encouraged him for a while in London. She couldn't understand why he didn't get it done. Laziness, that's why. She doesn't understand self-indulgence or procrastination. It isn't in her DNA.

It was an outdoor concert, on a hot summer night in 1947, at Kibbutz Ein Harod, near Gideon's Cave, where fresh water springs feed a cool pool in the parched Jezreel Valley. People drove from miles around in trucks and farm vehicles to hear Bernstein conduct; he was like a god to that generation. Yossi's mother Frieda was sixteen, his father David eighteen. Sitting next to each other in the summer dust, Frieda's parents began talking to David's parents, weeping when they realised that they came from nearby villages in devastated Poland.

Frieda and David had to stand throughout the concert. Frieda said David had supported her, allowed her to lean on him as she grew tired. They'd all had to sleep in their trucks afterwards because of security restrictions on travelling. A year later, when Israel became a state, Yossi's parents declared their love and became engaged during the celebrations.

And had a long, settled life together.

Taking out of his desk drawer the programme from the concert, which his mother had cherished, he carefully unwraps the tissue paper. His dearest possession. Yellowed, ragged, well-thumbed, the thin, friable paper is getting brown spots. The lovely, old-fashioned Hebrew.

Tucked inside the programme there are a few black and white photos he sourced years ago from the archives. Bernstein conducts, looking like a matinee idol in his white jacket and black bow tie, so young, with his brooding good looks, his impossibly long fingers. Behind him sit the crowd, serious, gaunt, young also.

The sunshine beckons and, when he's finished his coffee, Yossi grabs his stuff and walks across the road to Cornwall Park, listening to The Strokes on his iPod. He's walked miles since he got here, exploring the city. No dark underground and jostling with a million others, no claustrophobic tunnels, no paranoid glances at dodgy looking characters with backpacks. Sometimes he sees only four or five other people all the way around this park.

It's quiet and warm as he walks through the trees with their gracious English feel, then over the cattle stops and up One Tree Hill, smiling at dogs and young children and gorgeous women running and walking in groups of two and three, looking prosperous and fit. From the top of One Tree Hill, just fifteen minutes walk from their home, he can see the whole Auckland isthmus, where he and more than a million others live on a giant, volcanic field that could, in theory, spew basalt magma at any time.

He loves it up here. The three hundred and sixty degree views.

The extravagant blister and burst of explosion craters, scoria crowns, and hardened lava ridges. Green everywhere, swathes of parks and gardens. Woven among them in the distance, would-be skyscrapers that come nowhere near the sky, straggling motorways, ugly industry, toy-town housing, striding bridges. Not to mention water, water, water. Two sprawling harbours and countless bays and inlets join with the sky to dwarf the small bits of land and human endeavour in between.

And, although Claire talks as though her country lacks history, up here, amongst the grass, he can touch and stand on the mossy, sun-warmed remains of Māori fortifications, which once must have had the best view of approaching enemies. Not ancient, but fascinating. Māori had lived so lightly on this land.

He sets off down the hill again. Every person he passes smiles and says good morning. It reminds him of home, of Israel. Lovely. He instructs his iPod to play Bernstein conducting his Jeremiah Symphony. Tries not to waggle his head too much and look weird. Da da dum da da dum. Perfect, beautiful. Lamentations for the destruction of Jerusalem. Dedicated to Bernstein's father. They'd played this at the concert at Ein Harod that he is writing about.

He can go deep with this article, if he has the courage. The contrast between the socialist, secular dream his parents had cherished and the Israel they now had. Growing up under siege. Their pride in the lush valley, with its fragrant eucalyptus trees, transformed from the arid land they had found.

He wants to settle as his parents did. To offer Roimata the stability he had. He wants to spend the rest of his life with Claire. Should he cook traditional Israeli food for their wedding? Or summer barbeque food?

After the park, he'll head to the fish shop in Mt Eden, call at Time Out Bookstore, buy some vegetables at the Chinese market. He's been pampering Claire and Roimata: fish broth with dumplings, pasta with goat's cheese and rocket, spicy lamb with artichokes. This is the life.

When he gets back to Epsom he puts snapper fillets, crisp iceberg lettuce, red onions, feta cheese and a pottle of gourmet ice-cream in the fridge. He resists tearing a bit off the crusty ciabatta.

He sits down at his desk again. Today he wants to concentrate on the selection of music for the concert. Schumann Symphony no 2. Chosen because it's about triumph over adversity? There's a thematic tribute to the Ode to Joy. Joy. What did that mean to holocaust survivors? What does it mean to him?

Ravel's Piano Concerto. His darling Argerich is renowned for it. His mother had played a recording of the *Adagio* at his father's funeral and told the story of their meeting. Painfully beautiful. To this day he can hardly bear to listen to it.

How he misses his dear parents. David, killed in the Yom Kippur War. Frieda, dead five years later of the cancer she believed was caused by heartbreak.

If he talks about these things, perhaps Claire will open up too. Maybe she will tell him about her childhood. She needs to move on. He must make her. If he talks about why he left Israel, why he is so afraid of returning there, whether he ought to feel ashamed, maybe she will feel it safe to talk? A person needs to deal with such issues, face them, and learn from their history, before they can go ahead with their lives.

6

LONDON 1995

CLAIRE HAS NEVER FELT LOVE like it. In snatched moments of sleep she dreams she's a snarling tiger, making a burrow under their Camden house, lining it with blankets, rough on Roimata's downy skin. She doesn't want clean at first. Doesn't want fresh or new or shop-bought. Just close. And natural. Natural, a word the old Claire had hated. An over-used, misunderstood, advertising-mangled word. The new Claire is overawed by natural.

About this time Claire reads a fable about a Japanese gardener who grows five thousand orchids and, on the day the Emperor is to visit, cuts them all away but for one perfect flower. What a silly story. But when she protects Roimata beneath her shoulder while she suckles, Roimata is like that one orchid; she would step over five thousand babies to save this one. A fierce war-like Claire emerges each day, dressed for battle in huge vomit-stained t-shirts and floppy track pants.

Claire always finds intimacy tiring, like speaking a foreign language. Not with Roimata. Deluged with hormones, she drinks in the baby's jungle smells, duckling fluff skin, *umami* tears. After a while, one sight of Roimata's fat wrists wiggling their way out of the tight, soothing wrap after sleep can inspire a whole frenzy of cleaning, washing and imposing order on their lair; all the while Roimata and she carry on this ancient dance of eye-contact: gaze, chuckle, gurgle, flirt, murmur, belly-laugh. Back and forth. She could do this forever.

Never has she said anything so worth saying as that operatic dawn "heeellloooo," her attuned voice finding the perfect pitch for love, sending Roimata the message: trust me, trust the world.

When Roimata is about six months old, Claire returns to work. She wriggles back in to her composure, pulling on her 'Doctor Bowerman' thick black tights and giggling when they make her think of stretch-and-grows. She hides how much this has changed her. When other staff kindly enquire after her baby they're met with a dismissive "she's meeting all her milestones" brush-off. She finds it embarrassing, this overwhelming love for her baby. Why be so moved by something so common, so ordinary?

Work is difficult at first, cutting into perfect skin, especially if the child is a similar age to Roimata. The pain of the parents overwhelms her a few times. She teaches herself all over again that she can help them most if she remains detached. The last thing they need is her empathy. Her kindness, yes. All the energy of her intellect beamed on finding a surgical answer, yes. Her emotions? Not helpful.

Later, as Roimata grows, she never tires of hearing how much she is adored.

"I love every molecule of you."

"My snot? My vomit?"

"Even the gunge between your toes."

Or,

"I love you so much I could pop."

"Go on then, pop."

"Cheeky rabbit."

7

AUCKLAND 2010

The lift from the surgical ward up to oncology is bright yellow with lots of glass. It glides up through the soaring atrium, past levels painted baby-boy blue, Barbie pink and sickly apricot. They got the apricot wrong. No-one's liked that colour since her Nana's generation. Claire can look down on a scruffy rainforest-themed playground on a bed of leaf-patterned lino but she's looking at patient notes instead.

Her friend Sam has asked her to see a family this morning.

"They're serious hippies. Well, Mum is. We had to work hard to get them to consent to chemo but he's had ten weeks of it now. The tumour's shrunk well."

Sure enough, she notices the child hasn't had any immunisations and hasn't even been allowed his Vitamin K injection at birth. She stops in the corridor to take one last look at the CT scan. Wilms' Tumour, a tumour on the kidney. Horribly frightening for families, of course, but they have huge success with surgery. If your child has to have cancer, this is the one to have. She will need to remove only the affected kidney.

She pauses outside Sam's door and shuts the folder. There's a yellow post-it note on the front, on which the department secretary has scribbled, *Rachel Rakena rang. Please call her.* The number's an Auckland one. She takes the note off and puts it in her pocket.

Sam, normally upbeat and cheery with patients, is a bit subdued when he opens the door.

"Claire, meet Rory. And Kate and Isa'ako Peteru."

Claire smiles a practised smile, warm enough to inspire confidence, but rueful enough to assure them that she knows it's a terrible time for them. Two-year-old Rory sits on his mother's knee, half-heartedly fiddling with a glittery My Little Pony.

"Hey Rory."

Mrs Peteru's corkscrew blonde curls bounce around as she talks. Too tall for the child's seat she's sitting in, all four of her slender limbs seem to grasp Rory. Claire stops beside the beautiful child and touches his arm on her way past to sit next to Sam. He hardly moves, just lifts his huge brown eyes to his mother's face. When Mrs Peteru moves to protect him with her shoulder Claire knows she's made a mistake touching him.

Sam asks a few questions and the mother answers. Dad answers none of the questions. He's Samoan, tall and solidly quiet. He, at least, has an adult's chair but he still looks acutely uncomfortable, wriggling and clearing his throat a lot. His huge hands fiddle with the fluffy daffodil-yellow bear the hospital gives every child.

"Now, Claire's a surgeon. She's here to talk about the operation."

The mother bristles and looks at her husband, sighing and lifting her eyebrows. He frowns, twisting the fur on the bear between two massive fingers.

"Mr and Mrs Peteru, the chemo's shrunk the tumour well and that's great but it will grow back if we don't cut it out. The good news is that this surgery's ninety percent effective."

"No," Kate Peteru says. "How can we put a two-year-old through that? We want to try waiting. We believe in natural healing and prayer."

"I understand how hard this is. But acting soon is important, while we have it small," Sam says.

"Please trust me. I would not even agree to do the surgery unless I was sure it was best for Rory," Claire says. She turns to the father deliberately as she asks if they have any further questions. He continues to look down at the floor.

Someone has to say it. She doesn't want them to feel worse, knows they are desperate. But Rory is a sick wee boy. It's her job to protect him. She takes a deep breath.

"There's one more thing. You mentioned massage. Deep

massage, such as traditional Samoan massage, on his tummy." She mimes deep tissue massage. "We don't recommend that for this kind of tumour. It's a lump, you see," she says cupping her hands in a shape like an orange, "and we don't want it to rupture. If this tumour breaks up, it can spread the cancer cells around in Rory's tummy, perhaps spread it to his other kidney."

The parents say nothing, both looking away.

The phone shrills as she reaches her desk. She picks it up, hoping it's Sam to say he's got consent. But a woman's rich voice says, "Kia ora Claire, it's Rachel Rakena here."

Shit. Claire puts the blue folder on her desk and sits down in her chair, bumping her leg hard on her desk as she does so.

"Did you receive my letter?"

"I did."

"You must have noticed how much your daughter looks like my Nanny."

Claire says nothing.

"I'd love to meet you to talk about this."

The woman sounds more hesitant now.

The office door opens and Sam bounces in, pretending to tear his hair out as he sits down in the chair opposite her desk.

"Please, come to my house. Can you give me your e-mail address?" Rachel says.

Sam starts playing with the bright pink felt gerbera that sits on the desk. The leg crossed over his knee jiggles rapidly. Claire puts out her hand and takes the flower from him, widening her eyes and smiling over the phone at him to try to calm him down.

"Um, ok." She gives Rachel her email address, even while she knows she will regret it. "I have to go now."

She presses the END button, holding on to it for a few seconds. Sam bursts out talking as soon as she hangs up.

"The woman's a nutcase."

"Sorry, pardon?"

"Mrs Peteru. She's saying no to Rory's surgery. There's some alternative guy she wants to talk to."

"Did you get a chance to talk to the dad?"

"He didn't say a word. She's a fruitcake. She's like a born-again. You should have heard some of the things she said."

"Sam, she thinks this is best. She loves that boy. People do far worse things around here."

"She's a bloody fruitcake."

She knows he is deeply compassionate really. He's just venting, knowing she will understand.

The smell of cooking beef drifts through the house. Yossi's using the barbeque in the courtyard of the townhouse they've rented.

"Yossi, you've been working on the garden," Claire says, looking around as she sets the wooden table. "Have you been sowing seeds?"

"Coriander, sunflowers, beans." He points out three tiny plots to her.

They had agreed to rent somewhere easy and low-maintenance in town and work on Ruby Bay as their home. But Yossi seems to make a home wherever he is. She loves this about him. It's so nice of him to take the trouble to serve them outside in the fresh, soft air.

"I can't believe it," says Yossi, arranging the steaks and vegetables in flamboyant stacks on three plates, dribbling them with jus. "In a couple of months we will be married."

"I want to be a bridesmaid," Roi says. "I've never been a bridesmaid."

Claire's struck again by Roimata's ease with this sort of thing, the 'girly' stuff, the 'social' stuff. Didn't get that from her mother.

"Well –" says Claire. Bridesmaids? Jesus. But she sees Roimata's happy face.

"When can we shop for your dress? We need to choose that first, before Debs and I pick ours."

"Do we? Hey Yoss, shall we just wear sarongs? Beach clothes?"

"No way. Mum, you always spoil things. Have some fun. Debs and I have decided. You're wearing a special dress. We both want a new dress too."

"I am having nothing to do with it. I'd marry you in your jeans," says Yossi.

"Debs and I think you should wear cream or buttery yellow. It always looks good with your brown eyes. You're so tanned and slim; you'll get away with it. We both look good in green. I love that dress Keira Knightley wears in Atonement."

Claire laughs.

"Hey, I want to wear that dress, if anyone's going to. Not sure it's very Waiheke though. Now go up and study, miss. Wedding or no wedding." She has to reach up to cuddle her beautiful daughter these days.

When it's dark and the mosquitoes start bothering them, they move into the kitchen. Claire checks her Inbox on her laptop. Yossi leans over and puts his arm around her, his breath hot on her cheek. He smells of garlic and smoke from the barbeque.

"My darling, are you ok?" he asks.

"Fine. Why?" She lowers the lid so he won't read her emails.

"You seem so unsure, so diffident here. At home, back in London, you were so –"

"I'm fine."

She's rescued by the kettle boiling.

From Sam. *Re: Peteru case. (Wilms' tumour.) Help. Mother more hostile than ever. Angry over the Samoan massage thing. I think I've persuaded her to come in at 11am tomorrow. Hope you can be there too.*

One from Rachel Rakena. She's insisting Claire meets with her. This woman's a force of nature. Claire deletes it. Thank goodness she got to it before Yossi saw it. She'll see this woman, for Roi's sake. But she needs to think. She wants to get used to the idea herself before she tells Yossi or Roi. How can she protect them all?

8

"THERE ARE CASES WHERE SURGICAL intervention is rather a subjective decision, but this is not one of them," Sam's saying as Claire nudges her way into the small meeting room, which is bursting with people, some leaning against the walls.

He sounds defensive. Not surprising really; instead of the usual four or five people at the case meeting, there are clinical leaders, managers, extra social workers, the communications manager, and lawyers for the hospital. Everyone wants to get in on the Peteru drama.

Mele, the Samoan cultural advisor, stands and talks about the Peteru family's faith and their dignity.

"In the case of Samoan families, it may not be Rory's parents making this decision. Older family members may be in charge."

"Have you had a chance to talk to Isa'ako or any of the extended family members? Can we get them all together to get to the bottom of this?" Sam asks her.

"The mother's determined she does not want this. In the wider family, I would say there is disagreement. A minister in their church in Kelston is going to cure Rory by laying on hands."

Sam leans over as he whispers, "Bit hard to do randomised double-blind controlled trials on this one then." Claire fights back a laugh. That would not be a good look.

"Can Sam and I meet with some of the family?" she says.

"The mother says there's no point in any more meetings."

"What does the Dad think?"

"It's hard to say. With all these women in his ear."

There's laughter. A pākehā social worker with thinning hair

introduces herself in a long Māori greeting, telling them her name, her origins, her mountain, her river.

"Love the earrings," Sam whispers to Claire. Claire frowns at him, but he's right. Her earrings are ridiculous. Bright plastic beads in a huge cascade, they rattle every time she moves. This and her baggy t-shirt and elastic-waisted skirt are not encouraging Claire to take this woman seriously.

"Samoan people believe that illness is caused by evil gods." She speaks slowly and looks pained, as though she's talking to two-year-olds, or perhaps talking about a sacred text delivered to her personally on a mountain by a fiery angel. She struggles for words. She's the only one who can possibly understand it, clearly. Preserve us. Claire would far rather be able to communicate with the parents directly.

"And if we don't force them to do surgery?" a manager interrupts. Thank goodness, someone practical.

"Based on observation of animals and on children in Third World countries with untreated tumours, it will almost certainly grow again. It can be fatal," Sam says.

Claire's pager buzzes again. She looks at her watch. They need her upstairs. She stands and apologises. She has to go, speaks before she thinks. "The actual issue here is who gets to make the decision. I have no doubt Mrs Peteru is sincere but, the fact is, she's making an irrational choice. It's a life and death matter for this boy and we should compel them to come in for the surgery. The parents can be with him pre and post, but must be relieved of their legal custody for the few hours of surgery." She's on her way out. She's told them what she thinks. It's not her decision.

The social worker jumps to her feet again.

"Well I think that would be a real mistake. The public would be outraged. Who are we to know better than his own parents?"

Claire's at the door. She can't resist a parting shot.

"Weighing up the harm of being seen as arrogant versus Rory dying, I'm willing to look bad." She could have said that more kindly. The best thing for everyone will be if Sam can talk Rory's parents into having the surgery. It's all about relationship.

But the Peterus don't turn up for their appointment.

"I'm going to go to their home. They're in Point Chev. You don't have time to come with me, do you? I want to meet her on her own turf and make her see reason," Sam says.

She's flattered he's asked. She knows relationships are not her strong point.

"Of course. My registrars can cope. The last thing we want is to have to involve the law."

Just before lunch, they head out there. The Peteru house is a 1920s bungalow in a long flat street of similar houses. When Claire left Auckland, this was a poor white area. Now it's full of young families, middle-class, and fashionable. People here eat organic food, drive mid-price cars, join babysitting clubs and cycle to work. Many don't immunise their children. The bungalows are painted designer colours and, although from the street they still look like small workers' cottages, most owners have pushed the back out to add light-filled kitchens and family rooms.

"Shared driveways," Sam says as he parks the car. They both grimace. In-fill housing has squashed an ugly modern kitset house right behind the homely green bungalow. The driveway goes on past that house to even more houses. Children get run over in driveways like these.

As soon as Claire and Sam walk onto the property a cute girl wearing only knickers and a pink helmet drops her plastic bike and runs around the back of the house. They step up on to the porch with its neat white balustrade. Children's jandals in various sizes and colours line up neatly beside the door, alongside a huge pair of men's black Havaianas.

"You do the talking," Claire says as she knocks.

Kate Peteru has a bright green and blue lava-lava tied around her slender waist and she wears a plain t-shirt, but she still manages to look haughty.

"Hi, Kate. You didn't come to your appointment. How's Rory?" Sam says.

"He's fine." She stands one hand on the door frame, the other firmly on her hip. No invitation to come in.

"Can we take a look at Rory while we're here?" Sam says.

"We're trying other treatments."

"Mrs Peteru, can we please talk?" He's being too gentle.

"My naturopath's got a machine that uses Rory's natural energy, it boosts it, increases the healing. I don't want you cutting into Rory." She begins to shut the door.

Claire steps forward, holds the door open. "Mrs Peteru – I know it's hard."

"We don't want your surgery." Kate pushes to shut the door.

"Rory is really ill." Sam speaks quietly. "Mrs Peteru, if you don't consent, we'll start proceedings to force you. Please show up at the hospital at seven tomorrow morning. Make it easy on all of us. Give Rory a meal soon and then give him nothing to eat or drink until his surgery is over."

"We'll think about it."

She shuts the door.

Driving to the hospital, she and Sam talk the case over and work out their plan of action.

"Thanks, heaps, Claire. Lots of surgeons wouldn't get involved like this," says Sam. "But you're so supportive."

"I hope we're doing the right thing."

Surgeons have to believe in themselves. They have to be confident. How else would you cut into others' bodies?

9

YOSSI

Every ten minutes or so another person asks the lady on the desk about researching family history. She replies patiently in an accent Yossi thinks is South African, directing them to ships passenger lists, electoral rolls, marriage registers. Yossi tries not to listen. He's working here to avoid getting distracted and procrastinating at home.

He scrolls down the memoir that an archivist in Tel Aviv has sent him. This woman arrived in Israel on the same boatload of illegal immigrants as Yossi's mother, Frieda, both teenagers at the time. His mother had her parents with her, but this poor woman had arrived alone. As he reads of her hunger on the overcrowded boat, he hears his mother's voice, cracked, tough, full of Yiddish humour. Landing on the coast at night, they'd been smuggled into the countryside and hidden from the English. The old lady wrote of waking up dirty, skinny and illegal, and looking out of the window at orange groves.

I thought I must have been shot by the British soldiers and gone to heaven. I walked outside and it was sunny. My host handed me a cut-up orange. "Shalom," he said. When I bit into the juicy, sharp fruit, I knew I was going to be all right. I cried. I had lost my parents, my grandparents, my sister, but I was here. I was alive.

Yossi's legs ache. His eyes blur. He gets up, goes for a walk around the rest of the first floor. Stretches, checks his phone. It's ten o'clock. He should work another hour at least before he goes for coffee. A display at the end of a row of shelves catches his eye.

Bright red letters, stuck above a selection of books, read FAMOUS NEW ZEALAND MYSTERIES. He glances around. No-one is looking at him. He takes one of the books off its metal stand. *Into Thin Air – Unsolved New Zealand Mysteries.* On the front a young woman laughs, her hair an iridescent halo. She's superimposed on a sketch of a car and a shadowy man on a lonely road.

He glances at the Table of Contents. There it is, *Chapter 4, Kathryn Phillips (Cover story).* Is that the one? Sure enough, the chapter is illustrated with two photos. The girl from the cover. And a police mug-shot of a man. Dark hair, even features, hostile eyes. The name underneath confirms Yossi's suspicions.

The disappearance of pretty hitchhiker Kathryn Phillips on 27th February 1970 has never been solved. The seventeen-year-old from Manurewa was on her way to her sister's twenty-first party in Taumarunui. Her brother watched her set off in a red dress, with a backpack, relaxed and excited about her trip.

Yossi closes the book and looks around. He takes it to the table and gathers up his stuff, hiding the lurid cover in the middle of his pile. He'll use the self-checkout machine.

10

Rachel Rakena's Mt Eden villa is crammed with books and Māori artifacts. Patu, taiaha, kete and waka huia pose on tables and shelves, alongside travel mementoes: a small concrete Buddha, a terracotta army soldier and Venetian masks. Framed family photographs stare from the long narrow hallway. Rachel explains that she lives here on her own, was divorced a long time ago and has no children of her own. She's a high school principal and books and papers spill from an armchair onto the floor. Even at home in the evening she's well groomed, her grey bob swinging in perfect shape, her solid body sheathed in a flattering black dress. She's kicked off her shoes and her plump brown legs and feet are bare.

Claire feels scruffy and sweaty and worn. She mumbles an apology, explains she's come straight from work.

"Your work is so important," says Rachael. "You're a fantastic doctor. Our whānau is so grateful."

"Thank you."

The dark red lounge has doors that are open to a small but glorious cottage garden. She and Rachel walk around it, Rachel picking a bunch of flowers for Claire as they go. White roses tangle with jumbles of yellow dahlias. Blue lavender, Queen Anne's lace and tiny white alyssum fill in the gaps. It reminds Claire of her piano teacher's garden when she was a child. There's no lawn, just a riot of flowers with a sweet path of pebbles meandering through, which make a pleasing crunch as Rachel and Claire wander.

"You must be so busy in your job. How do you keep a garden like this?"

"I love it, it's my stress relief. I have heaps of whānau staying with me. They send me the naughty ones. I put them all to work," Rachel laughs.

Claire finds herself sipping a glass of wine in the lounge. The smells of the garden surround them. At one end a wall is covered by an enormous framed poster for the Te Māori exhibition at the Met, featuring a huge glowing greenstone hei tiki, minimally lit against a dark background so that it seems to hang in mid-air. On another, a black and white photo of an elderly Māori woman follows her with beady eyes, feather cloak draped around her straight shoulders, chin held high. Rachel tells her it's her Nanny Roimata. As if she didn't know. It's her Roi, with wrinkles. Like one of those photos they alter with computers now, to predict how missing children will look years later.

Claire's tired. She wants to deny the truth and get out of here. Rachel's way of putting her at ease brings memories of the easy conversation she'd had with Brent Te Hira in Italy. A class act, this family.

"She was amazing, our Nanny," says Rachel.

Here it comes. A lecture about Roimata's Māori background and her need to know her whakapapa. She's right, of course. Claire sighs to herself and settles back in the chair. Instead Rachel reaches for an album and points out photos. Nanny Roi in front of a meetinghouse with a beehive hairdo. Then surrounded by scruffy teenagers with Afros and stripy t-shirts.

"That's when she helped start an urban marae."

Next one of a group of women in hats and gloves.

"She was high up in the Māori Women's Welfare League. Look, there she is with Dame Whina Cooper."

Welcoming Prince Philip with a hongi in the seventies.

"She was so proud of that one. She loved the Royals."

There are many where Roimata stands surrounded by children, usually in front of the same weatherboard state house. She's a snappy dresser – fitted dresses and matching shoes.

"Where's that?" Claire asks Rachel.

"G.I."

"G.I.?" Claire asks, confused.

"Glen Innes. She brought up lots of grandchildren in that house. Me and Brent and lots of others. Boy she could be bossy. But she was a strong woman."

Sounds like her Roimata. "I assume you think there's at least a chance Roimata is related to me or you wouldn't be here?"

Claire straightens up and puts her wine glass down on the coffee table. Rachel touches her arm, keeping her seated.

"Claire, I know more than you think. My brother, Brent, who lives in Germany told me he'd met a woman at the urupā, the graveyard where our Papa Donald lies."

She hands Claire a photo of a young man with cornrows, in a white shirt and black leather jacket, standing in front of the Eiffel Tower. He's beautiful. So young. A stranger to her, really.

"He described you to me. I'm sure Claire was the name. Petite. Pretty. A doctor." Holding her hands in front of her, with each word she taps a different finger, like a lawyer arguing a case.

Claire stares at the photo. He's smiling intimately at whoever's behind the camera.

"I –" Claire is lost for words.

"He was confused," Rachel says. "Wondered if it meant he no longer loved his wife, Marita. They were having a hard time. I helped Marita look after the children in Berlin while he went off to Italy for the rugby trip. He was stressed out."

A mosquito whines and it prompts Rachel to shut the doors as dusk hovers. She switches on a lamp. The red walls glow and the rose and gold Turkish rugs make the room feel like a cocoon. The garden has disappeared and the doors reflect the room now.

"Why did you call your daughter Roimata?"

Claire's head aches. She sips more wine. Its fruity taste overwhelms her. Rachel reaches across and takes her hand and she feels herself stiffen at the invasion of her space.

"It's ok, Claire. It's ok. It's a joy to me, to have found her. She's my flesh and blood."

Claire swallows. She knows she has to do this for Roimata. She's hated having to dodge her questions all those years. Hated knowing lately that Roi's given up asking.

"You named her after my Nanny, right?"

Silence. Claire wipes her eyes.

"Look, what do you want from me?" she asks Rachel.

"Nothing, Claire. Nothing." She strokes Claire's hand some more.

More silence.

"He talked a lot about his grandmother Roimata. And his grandfather, buried there in Italy, only seventeen. Left her pregnant back here. It was so sad. I had an irrational thought about giving the baby her name while I was pregnant, and it just stuck." Claire's voice sounds far away to her.

"It means tears," Rachel says.

Claire nods.

"What have you told Roimata about her father?" Rachel asks.

"I've tried to tell her the truth. That it was a holiday romance. In the last few years, I've explained that he was married and how ashamed of that I am. That I'm so pleased she's here and I love her so much. That Yossi loves her like a father. It's the parenting that matters, not the genes."

"True. But blood's thicker than water."

Fear of what's to come surges through Claire.

As she leaves, Rachel hands her the flowers and tells her she can't wait to meet Roi. They step past the open front door, gleaming white in the moonlight, and onto the wrap-around verandah. The rasp of cicadas hits them.

"I'm going to ring Brent right this instant and tell him about your Roimata." Rachel glances at her watch. "Oh, I'll have to wait a couple of hours until he's up. He still lives in Germany. He's an engineer."

Claire stops still.

"No, no. What about his wife? I don't want to cause any trouble. It's pointless to hurt their marriage after all these years."

"Marita died a few years ago from breast cancer."

Claire almost trips on the concrete step down from the verandah. That wife was the reason Claire didn't have to tell Brent about Roimata, the reason Roi would never need to meet him. She turns to face Rachel who's still up on the verandah, silhouetted by the light spilling from the door.

"Still, I'd rather you waited. Please don't tell him. I'm not ready."

"But this is his daughter, Claire. His own flesh and blood. We've already missed fifteen years."

That bloody cliché again.

"Ok. Tell him. But please warn him to keep his distance. I want to take it slowly with Roi. She's at a vulnerable age. I haven't even told my partner, Yossi, that I'm meeting with you. He's been a father to Roi. Please, give me some time."

"Ok, Claire." Rachael smiles and nods. "Let me know when I can meet Roimata. It's going to be alright, you know. See you again soon."

She drives the few blocks home through streets familiar from a long time ago, past her old school where Roimata's now a pupil, past rows of wooden houses with leafy gardens, shadowy in the dark. The smell of the flowers on the seat beside her fills the car, almost too sweet. She winds down her window. Tries to imagine telling Roimata. Tries to have the conversation. It feels wrong. Anything I have to do with this family leaves me out of control, she thinks. This bloody country leaves me out of control.

11

AUCKLAND 1978

After biking home from netball, Claire runs a bath. She almost drops her Famous Five book in the water as she tries to keep reading and take off her netball top at the same time. She loves George so much. When she turns the tap off, she can hear Mum crying again. She wants Claire to go to her. Claire jumps in the bath instead.

When the book's finished, the water's cold. She gets out and dries herself. Mum must have heard her empty the bath because she starts crying out again. Claire picks her favourite butterfly dress and her shorts and top off her bedroom floor and puts them in the washing machine, so that she can wear them to school this week. Mum's wailing gets louder. She will go to her. In a minute.

She makes herself a peanut butter sandwich. Yum. Fresh bread she'd biked up to the dairy and bought this morning. She can't cut it very well but she quite likes the look of her uneven thick bits. She can pick the middle out. Mum won't tell her off because she's in a crying mood today.

What does her mother like? Cheese and pickle. Yuk, the pickle stinks. But her Mum loves it and it might cheer her up. She makes a cup of tea. As she opens her mother's door the sobbing gets so loud it hurts her ears.

There's a new axe beside Mum's bed. It has a shiny red handle. The cricket bat and the carving knife are still there too. Mum's standing on the window seat fiddling with the string trap she's set up so that if a man comes in through the window a pile of books will fall on to the floor and wake them up.

There's a knock at the front door.

"Hellooo, Claire, how are you? You all ready to come with me?"

It's a lady she's never seen before, wearing high purple platforms. Claire wants some platforms.

"You're coming with me to visit your dad."

The crying starts up again. Poor Mum.

"Hello-o. Mrs Bowerman? It's Joan Holt, from Social Welfare."

Her mother just howls louder.

"Claire, your mother's very unhappy about this I know. The court orders say your father is to spend some time with you. He's waiting at a nice place where parents and children can spend time together." She calls out. "I'll be with her the whole time to make sure she's happy and safe, Mrs Bowerman."

Court orders. Doesn't he want to spend time with her? Are they ordering him to?

"Watch out for her, Claire. She's on his bloody side. Don't listen to that murdering bastard."

Claire goes over and cuddles her. "It's alright Mum. I'll make you a nice dinner when I get home. I'll roast that chicken we got. You have a rest. Shhhh! I'll be fine, Mum."

Claire quickly shuts the front door behind her in case the neighbours hear the yelling. Mum shouldn't swear so much.

Claire can't remember going over the Harbour Bridge before. The city looks like Toy Town once they're right out in the middle, as they swoop over toy boats bobbing. Makes her feel a bit sick though, looking down so far.

"I feel like I'm flying all the way to Australia," says Claire.

"No, no. Australia's on the other side, out west. This sea's the Pacific, and it goes all the way to South America," the lady says.

She should have known that. She can feel her cheeks burning. She'll study her school atlas tonight and learn it all. She hates getting things wrong. Hot tears prickle.

When they arrive at an old house where there are other men

and kids, her Dad has tears in his eyes, too. He should be happy to see her. To distract him she sings the title music to The Muppets TV show. *It's time to get things started –*

He laughs.

They play Last Card, putting the cards on a sticky coffee table. Her father's no good at cards. She beats him every time. When she goes to the toilet the wees smell is awful, the water runs all brown and it looks dirty so she runs out again. She'll just hold on until she gets home.

"Now let's read about our favourite silly bear."

"I want to hear about Eeyore's birthday and the balloon."

Claire runs up the driveway, not stepping on the cracks, wondering whether her mother's stopped crying yet. She finds her in the kitchen. The chicken's in the oven, making the house smell yum.

"Hello darling. Dinner's all ready. Let's sit down together after that and watch some telly. Get Smart's on at five thirty. And I've made the trap better so we'll have a good sleep tonight. The night visitors won't bother us."

12

AUCKLAND 2010

Claire hears the clink of ice in a glass and Yossi's footsteps up the stairs to their bedroom. She covers herself with the thin sheet. Yossi has homemade lemonade for her in one hand and Rachel's flowers in a pretty vintage vase in the other. He puts both down on her bedside table.

"I brought these up to cheer you up. They're gorgeous. From a patient?"

She nods and takes a sip of the cool lemonade. God, she never lies to him. She needs to sort this.

"That's just great. Refreshing. Thank you."

"The lemons are from our tree," he says, stripping off his clothes until he's in just his blue and white boxers, his legs thin, tanned and muscly. He goes into their bathroom and then comes back into their room cleaning his teeth.

"Headache better?" he says in between brushing. "You shouldn't be working."

"Sorry," Claire says. "It's this case." She motions at the file, which she's been trying to study. "The Wilms' tumour I told you about. The parents are still not giving consent."

"That woman's not bad," he says, climbing into bed beside her. "She's just ignorant. She's angry at what is happening with her child."

"Why do people romanticise nature? Nature can be brutal," says Claire. "Cancer's natural. It will kill this wee boy. And bloody flaxseed oil will not help."

She leans over and turns off her bedside lamp. Turns her back on Yossi. He's switched his light off too, but he's reading on his iPad, which makes a glow around him. Claire closes her eyes and images of Rory's scan float behind her lids, the tumour smooth and round like a child's ball. She goes over and over the way she will cut. She doesn't know for sure whether she's doing the right thing. Who knows anything for sure? She refuses to do nothing.

It's stifling. Claire wriggles and stretches in bed. The sheets bunch and twist.

She'll have to tell Roimata about Brent. There's no way around it. How will she react? The flowers beside her bed smell heady, especially the spiky white Nicotiana. What will Yossi feel about Brent? It might hurt him a lot. He's been so good to Roi. Should she just refuse to have anything to do with Brent? His name's not on the birth certificate. He has no rights. God, could he insist on a paternity test or something hideous? She needs to avoid that sort of thing at all costs. Yossi's never formally adopted Roimata. Perhaps they should do that.

Kate Peteru's objection is based on some anti-scientific, airy-fairy notion of 'natural'. The father's harder, though. He says little. In broken English, he talks about prayer and about God's will. It's been hard to talk to him at all. Are she and Sam being racist? Paternalistic?

Roimata, her darling Roimata. What will this mean? Confusion? Danger? Divided loyalties. All things Claire's tried to protect her from.

When the sun comes up, her head is aching. She creeps out of bed and pulls on shorts and a t-shirt. She's decided to run to the hospital. She can shower when she gets there and wear scrubs. A run will clear her mind. She leaves Yossi a note. *Yoss, do you want to meet me for lunch? That café on Park Road at one o'clock?*

Birdsong and bright early sun. In the dry gardens, hibiscus flowers in a stunning variety of colours. Yellow dahlias and daisies are improbably showy. God she hopes the family will turn up for surgery. She knows these cases can explode.

She runs along Gillies Avenue, past her old high school. She'd had some fantastic teachers. They'd picked up early her ability at science, inspired and encouraged her. Mrs Springford, Mr Peters. She still remembers the ones who helped her to fall in love with learning.

One or two girls had told her straight out that their parents banned them from being friends with her because her father was a murderer. Some of the mothers were fascinated. They'd been ingratiating, over-friendly, excited. Being close to notoriety seemed to feel exciting to some people, as though they were close to fame. Looking back, she's not sure which is worse, the shunning or the perverted thrill.

One mother had even grilled her – trying to sound casual, she'd asked for lurid details. Where was her father on the day the young hitchhiker disappeared? Did her mother believe he was guilty? Claire remembers thinking: I'm fourteen, not four. I know what you are up to. She'd ended up lying. *He has an alibi, that's why the police had to free him.* This had shut the woman up, and the many others after her when Claire began to repeat it often. She even told her friends this, sometimes.

A Labrador bounds up to her, butting her legs, leaping about, slobber dripping from its mouth. She slows right down, turns side-on to it. It seems friendly enough but she looks around for an owner. A runner appears from a corner and calls the dog.

"Sorry," he says, smiling flirtatiously.

A mother had stopped her outside the school once, holding a huge black Labrador on a leash. *Claire, I'm psychic. The body of that poor girl is buried in a paddock with cows. I see it all the time. And if you bring me something of your father's, a piece of his clothing or something, I will be able to feel the vibrations and tell you whether he did it or not.*

Her friend had saved her, pulling on her arm. *Claire's been told not to talk about the case.* And walking away. Good old Anna, she'd been brilliant.

The run's helping now. Oxygen, endorphins, serotonin. The worn stone walls are spilling Mexican daisies, the pink and white flowers soft even in this bright sunrise. She'd had to run along this avenue almost every day when she was young. Groups of girls. Chattering like bright birds.

At seven, patients start arriving for simple, day-stay surgery. All she can think about is Rory. If the Peterus arrive in the next half hour, she'll do his surgery herself. Her registrars talk to families in the waiting room. She double checks the notes for each child, concerned that in the stress of this case, she might make a mistake somewhere else.

It's eight o'clock and the Peterus have not shown. The ward clerk tells her they're not answering their phone. She and Sam have a quick consultation with hospital management and clinical leaders who decide to call the police. Her headache is back with a vengeance, the bright coloured corridors shimmering.

13

YOSSI

"Bye, Yoss. Orchestra practice after school."

Roi gives him a hug as she rushes out the door. Over her shoulder he can see her muesli bowl abandoned on the table but decides not to say anything. He rinses it and puts it in the dishwasher. He knows he spoils her. It's a funny idea, this 'spoiling' a child.

Before he can start working on his article, he must go over the accounts his manager has sent. Claire had urged him to hold on to Blue Bike, because they might move back to London and then he would be glad he hadn't sold it. He'd loved the shop, but he's moved on really. Must do the accounts today. How boring. He scours the sink with Jif.

He opens the fridge. That's right, he bought those lamb cutlets yesterday. They'll be great tonight. Might even make mint sauce.

He goes to his bag, takes out the book and starts reading as he stands there. Looks again at the photo of Claire's father. His cheekbones are so like hers. Thick eyebrows arch over besieged eyes.

Her first ride was with a woman travelling to a rural farm near Pokeno, who said she dropped her at the side of State Highway 1. Kathryn Phillips was never seen again. The only clue police had was a possible sighting two kilometres further south, where an elderly couple saw a gold Holden Kingswood pull over and a girl in red climb in. The man remembered part of the registration, EN, because they happened to be his initials. While not a confirmed sighting, police believe it was likely to have been Kathryn Phillips.

Retired Detective Paul Royal, who led the investigation, says he will go to his grave thinking about this case. "It's a classic mystery, I guess, the way she just vanished. People all over New Zealand looked for her. We had reports of people as far away as Invercargill out searching their sheds and their land."

Print shop owner Patrick Bowerman, who owned a Holden Kingswood station wagon, registration EN998 was charged and convicted in 1975, five years after the murder.

1975. Claire must have been just five when he was arrested. The same age as Roi when they'd first come in to Blue Bike. Yossi remembers looking up from playing chess against himself to see Roimata's huge brown eyes staring at the chess set while she stood on tiptoes. The Berlioz *Vous Soupirez* duet filled the shop. Claire had loved it instantly. Perhaps they should play it at their wedding. She loves the way it is ardently romantic, yet still restrained and calm somehow.

Bowerman was sentenced to life imprisonment but in 1978 the Court of Appeal ordered a retrial and freed him on bail. He was convicted and jailed again twice, in 1979 then again on appeal in 1981. A Commission of Inquiry freed Bowerman in 1983 amid accusations police had falsified evidence and conducted a biased investigation.

1983. The year Yossi had fled Israel for London, halfway through his degree in Music. Hezbollah suicide bombings. The withdrawal of the peacekeepers from Lebanon. The crush of people on the crowded shuttle bus out to the old Terminal One at Ben Gurion. His fear as they took off.

A biased investigation? Here? Why would Claire not see her father then? He was pardoned.

The public and media, however, remained convinced that he was guilty. Arguably New Zealand's most hated man, Bowerman has always maintained his innocence but he has never accounted for his movements that fateful day.

"I think it marked a sort of end of innocence," says retired Sunday Times editor Bob Sanders. "In the years before this murder kids used to go out and enjoy themselves. It seemed such a free and safe country."

Yossi closes the book and stares at the cover. The sun is hot on his neck. It's the not knowing that's hard, she'd told him. As he presses on the corner of the book with his thumb, almost bending the hard cover, he's trying to hold two possibilities in his head. Not guilty, in which case Patrick had suffered unjustly, or guilty, which makes him a murderer and a liar. Claire, then, has a choice of two equally unpalatable roles: conspirator in ruining the man's life or sharing the genes of an evil bastard.

Surely this could be solved now?

His lovely Claire. She works so hard. She cares so much for others. The accounts can wait. He takes out some paper and begins to brainstorm for their wedding vows.

14

Claire's late and she almost runs across the road. The café's noisy and hot but the smells of coffee and home baking beckon. Yossi's ordered gazpacho for them both. He tells her he's just cycled through the Domain and he glows and talks about the gracious oak trees. He's been working on their wedding vows and he unfolds a scrappy bit of refill and begins to read. She's so tense. She needs to tell him. She interrupts him, ignores his hurt look.

"Yoss, they're lovely. We'll look at them at home. Sorry. But there's something we need to – I need to tell you – while Roi's not here –"

The coffee machine spurts and hisses. Claire's squashed into a chair with her ear right beside the noisy beast. The barista clatters and bangs as he performs his show. Lunchtime traffic roars outside each time the lights change to green, just a couple of metres from the open door of the café. They're straining to hear each other.

"A woman approached me at work. She knew I had a daughter called Roimata."

While she's telling him about Rachel Rakena, showing him the photos of Nanny Roimata and Brent, Yossi drops his spoon. Gazpacho splatters across the wooden table and into the sugar. He snatches his cellphone out of the way. Some drops of the thin red soup flick up onto his white t-shirt.

"Shit." He dabs at it with a paper napkin. "I can't believe you didn't tell me before." He closes his eyes, takes a deep breath, runs his thin fingers through his hair roughly, sits up straighter then looks at Claire again. Smiles.

"Of course, we must tell her. She has the right to know. It's simple," he says, then, catching the waitress walking past, and handing her his half-empty bowl of gazpacho. "Excuse me, this is not cold enough. Can you add some ice? And we ordered coffee. Where is it?"

"We will tell her tonight," he says to Claire.

"No, not yet. She's still getting used to her new school," says Claire, glancing at the poor waitress.

"It's too important to wait."

"Why?" Claire asks him. "I don't know a thing about this man."

He winces and she can hear how negative she sounds.

"It will be great for her to get to know her Māori side. I was thinking of following it up, but this is better. Her own family."

He sounds like the social workers at the hospital. Why does everyone go on about family? Claire and Yossi are Roimata's family. But she knows he's right.

"She's been asking me a bit about it, actually," Yossi says. "It's been an issue at school. They keep asking her to join some group. A few things have happened. Everyone she meets comments on her English accent and her Māori looks."

"She hasn't told me any of this."

"I think she feels I may have some understanding. I look different. My accent. She's questioned me a lot about being Israeli since we got here. I think this will help her, Claire."

The noise of the café grows even louder as a group of theatre nurses Claire knows come in chattering and laughing. One of them is looking at Yossi with curiosity. They're probably amazed anyone can love her; they think she's so hard. Let them think it. She needs them to follow her instructions in theatre, needs them to take her seriously and have trust in her as a surgeon.

"You're her father, not him. You've done all the hard work. You love her so much."

"Of course I am." He sounds snappy. "I know I love her and she loves me. It would be easy to feel jealous of him. And not just about Roimata." Claire looks down at her coffee. "But it's best for her."

The queue for the counter is backing up and people are standing right beside their table, bumping Claire as they jostle for space.

"It's not one of those bloody shows on television where they connect people up with family they have lost. Where it ends with the meeting and we're meant to think it's all happy ever after," is all she can muster. She's trying to sound like the old Claire, the London Claire, the skeptical Claire. But she just sounds bitter. This is just the start. Can't Yossi see that? There'll be people and demands and drama. Can't they just leave them alone?

"It's her choice," says Yossi. "Don't worry, Claire. It's going to be great."

He's always so bloody optimistic. Her mobile phone rings. It's Sam. The noise of the café almost drowns him out.

"Where are you?" he asks.

"Why? New case?"

"No. The Peterus. They've been given an ultimatum, but they've gone to the media."

That dear little boy. As if being so sick is not enough. Now he's caught in the middle of an adult drama.

"See you there in a minute," she tells Sam.

Yossi jumps on his bike while she waits to cross the road, fanning herself with a folder of notes. As he leaves, shouting a bit, he tells her he's listening to Tchaikovsky on his iPod and how much he loves it. "Pom, pom, pom," he sings, waggling his head. He's daft.

She watches him weave in and out of the lunchtime traffic, across Grafton Bridge, where workmen are reinforcing the high sides that prevent suicides plunging to the motorway below, past the leafy old colonial graveyard, where the homeless gather to drink. He turns right and she knows he will cycle down into the city to the air-conditioned library, to work on his Ein Harod article. Old-fashioned Yossi. He'd said it would be quiet there. He'll be humming along to his iPod, at peace with the world. In spite of what she's just told him. How can he do that?

A man starts to cross even though the light is red. Brakes squeal and horns toot as he dodges traffic. Wearing faded pyjama pants and a t-shirt with damp armpits and a sweat pool on his back, he shouts at the cars. When will the crossing signal turn green? Hurry up. The last thing she needs is to have to resuscitate the man in the filthy street. She will, of course, if he needs it. But he makes it to the other side and through the hospital gate.

Claire remembers the agony Yossi had expressed when Roimata had been due in King's Cross Station, on the way to a violin lesson, just an hour after the bomb exploded. His love was no different from hers, no different from it would have been had he shared DNA with Roimata. He'd wept for what might have happened and resolved to move his family to a peaceful place. Like her, he would throw himself in front of a train for this girl.

As for the bomb, an hour's no closer than three hours or thirty hours. Their chances of being in the wrong place at the wrong time were negligible. Yossi is irrational, but she understands his fear. Then he'd claimed the moral high ground, telling her some of what he had seen as a soldier. He wanted out of London. Anti-Israeli feeling was fermenting. Wherever he went, he sensed resentment and hostility. Her New Zealand passport seemed like a dream answer to him. And she loved him, she wanted him to be happy. She had told herself to try trusting him. Perhaps he was right, and perhaps it was time she got over her running away. So she'd come with him.

At last the traffic stops for a red light. Stepping out, she weaves in front of an idling bus. She peers around the side of it, about to run across. Just in time she sees a motorbike bearing down on her. She jumps, and the bike roars past her with a blast of fumes. Finally she can run, over another lane of traffic then across to the other side, into the cool shade from the hospital building.

15

YOSSI

Up in the New Zealand Room it's cold after the gorgeous sunshine outside. They're overdoing the air-conditioning. Yossi goes to the desk where a plump woman is tapping away on her computer.

"I'm interested in the case of a missing girl. Kathryn Phillips. She disappeared in 1970. I've checked on the Internet. There's nothing much. I guess the case is too old. Would you have any files here?"

Without saying anything, she leaves through a doorway behind her. Yossi watches a group of people at one table doing research together. They must be a genealogy club or something. They're loud, inconsiderate. The librarian brings two cardboard cartons. Ripped corners threaten to spill the contents. File boxes, scrapbooks, battered ring binders with stiff fastenings and curling covers, rolls of microfiche, yellowing papers with old-fashioned type. The only free table is next to the loud group. As he puts the boxes down on the table one of them reads out a description of one of her forbears to her friend. "I think she might have been a lady of the night." They both laugh.

Yossi looks through the boxes, picking up clippings randomly. He handles them gingerly. Stories about the disappearance, headlines calling it *The End of Innocence*. Opinion pieces debate whether the victim contributed by dressing provocatively and hitchhiking. A couple of articles about Patrick. The theory he had been having an affair with his receptionist, which his wife had discovered around the time of the disappearance. He was an alcoholic, claimed the newspaper, and he regularly drove up and down to Hamilton on business. If that was evidence, thousands of people could be tried for the murder, claimed another.

There was extensive coverage of the original trial. This is a good place to start.

Patrick Bowerman chose not to appear and offered no alibi for the day in question. None was required, his lawyers argued. The burden of proof was on the prosecution. But the case was weak at first glance. It all hinged on the partial number plate and on his being absent from work that day. No bloodstains in the car. Yossi wonders how good forensic evidence was back then. Or whether they could still test anything now. That would be something Claire would trust.

The jury was out for a sensational three days and arrived at a guilty verdict. The Commissioner of Police said the streets were safer for young women after this conviction. The moral right argued New Zealand was going to the dogs.

Yossi sits still, paper everywhere, too much to read. He senses the women at the next table staring at him. Has he made a noise or something? Claire, Claire, Claire. It seems real to him now, in a way it never has before. He sees her hurt, the way she holds it like a highly volatile chemical, never disturbing it even by a breath. Some of his friends think her cold; he thinks her resilient. When she is warm, she's fierce and loyal. If only he could tell her that her father was innocent, she would relax and she could let herself be happier.

The women next to him are laughing again. He packs all the papers back in the box. Can't get them in fast enough. Everything seems to be breaking down. Ripped punch-holes. Newspaper clippings that don't want to fold up again properly. He puts the two boxes on the unattended front desk, and goes straight to the Men's Room. Can't wait to wash his hands.

16

The CEO's office at the top of the old part of the hospital has a meeting table and a wide view of the harbour.

"Just as you predicted, the Peterus have complained about arrogant doctors. They're talking to journalists. I've banned all media from the hospital grounds. Who's the best person to front for the hospital?" Meryl says.

The communications manager seems about twenty-five and she oozes confidence. "I think you should, Meryl. It must come from the top."

Claire whispers to Sam that she's too perky by far but when he laughs, Claire feels bad. She wants to remind Miss Perky that they must, in every interview, show compassion for the family, who are doing what they think is right, but she can't think how to say this without seeming patronising.

"I want you to know that this family truly believe in what they are doing. This is not neglectful, not careless. These parents really love this boy. They just don't believe in us. They are protecting him," Claire says.

"So, if it's not neglectful, why are we taking out this order?" asks the young manager.

"We believe there is evidence that this is best for this child. It's a big call. We must remember that."

Anyway, Claire knows she's not the best one to front for the hospital. Her phone beeps to remind her about a case meeting. As she hurries out, she undertakes to discuss with her Head of Surgery and their staff the need to prepare and be ready to operate on Rory at a moment's notice. That's her job.

She races to the Starship building, glancing through the file for the next meeting. Che MacKenzie. Aged six. Four admissions to hospital with suspicious injuries. Yesterday she'd removed his spleen after trauma to his abdomen. A punch or a kick, she'd bet on it. The mother said he'd fallen down some stairs. Old, untreated fractures on the x-rays tell a different story. Claire hasn't met the mother; the boy's been alone whenever she's seen him. They need evidence though. Proof.

Someone's taken quite a good history recently. Aged six, he's moved from family member to family member to friend. Now with his mother.

In the corridor to the meeting room she catches up with Janet, and has a rant to her. "Meeting after bloody meeting. If this whānau had the answers, they would have been sorting it by now, like the other whānau we deal with. He has glue ear, he's not immunised, and his language is delayed. What do people have to do to kids in this country before we do something?"

"Careful," Janet warns her. "These families are bloody complex."

"All families are complex. We can't just let them keep hurting him. Someone has to do something."

"We don't have a great record when we take them away either. If we had somewhere perfect to send him —"

This is true too. Involving the authorities is no guarantee of improving life for any child.

Claire doesn't get the chance to decide whether to say her piece or not. Just a few minutes into the meeting, her pager summons her to theatre. Acute surgery on an eighteen-month old who's been run over in her parents' driveway. Another one. Horrible, but she's relieved to focus on the part of the job she loves. As she scrubs, she sheds the outside world.

For two hours she focuses on stopping bleeding, repairing, delicately stitching in the clean theatre. It's real, tangible, measurable, evidence-based. But she can't stop thinking about vulnerable Che. She's not a social worker, she tells herself sternly. What would she know about family? Let the rest of them decide.

On the news that night the lead story is the Peteru family. Claire's rushing to get to Sam's birthday dinner but Yossi calls her to watch, hands her a fragrant peppermint tea then stands with his arm around her. On screen some gentle, softly spoken guy hooks Rory up to a ridiculous machine he calls a 'booster'. Then the family prays with their minister.

"*Western medicine's just one more belief system,*" some academic is saying.

"Yeah, yeah, let's get a nun to do your surgery," Claire says to the television.

There's a shot of Claire driving her old Audi out of the hospital, with sunglasses on. They manage to make her look like a celebrity appearing in court or something. The reporter says she has no comment.

… Dr Claire Bowerman is the daughter of Patrick Arthur Bowerman, who was convicted of the murder of Kathryn Phillips, a hitchhiker who disappeared in 1970 near Pokeno. He was later pardoned.

That photograph. The smiling radiant girl. Still so familiar. They cut to a grainy still photo, a bewildered looking twelve-year-old Claire standing outside the High Court with her mother and father, both of them coiled and tense, like cats watching prey. There's a strong likeness between Patrick and Claire, something to do with their bone structure. Rita, smiling like the Queen, firmly grasps her daughter's shoulder.

Yossi mutes the TV as they move on to the next story.

Roi comes downstairs.

"Mum, what's happening? Charlotte texted me to say you were on TV."

"Roi, I'm sorry. There's a child at work. He's sick and his parents don't want us to treat him. It's got out into the media now."

"Why don't they want you to treat him?"

"It's complicated. They're protecting him because he's been through a lot. They are hoping that they can cure him with more natural things."

"Has anyone asked him what he wants?"

"He's only two."

"Will the surgery make him better?"

"Well, there's no guarantees. But there's a good chance."

"Will it make him worse?"

"There's a small risk. The risk from the cancer is far greater, so we have to make a call here."

Roi holds out her phone. "Hey Charlotte and I saw this dress today. We thought it was perfect for you for the wedding."

On the phone there is a photo of a buttery cream dress with a matching jacket sitting over the top. The sleeves are see-through and they have been embroidered with small birds and bird cages.

"Roi, it looks gorgeous. Thank you so much. Did they have the right size?"

"Yes. We'll need to try it on as soon as you have time. I'll get them to put one on hold."

"Oh yes, it looks so nice. I've got to change to go out to Sam's dinner now." Claire starts to move upstairs.

Roi comes with her and supervises her getting ready. She chooses a blue cotton dress and some vintage high shoes that Claire bought on a whim years ago and never wears. She makes Claire sit on the bed, pulls out the clip holding her hair, brushes and straightens the hair expertly, massaging her scalp to cheer her mother up.

"Now, look in the mirror," Roi says, with a final flourish of hairspray.

Who's that sleek creature staring back at her? Roimata's transformed her.

"Darling Roi-Roi bird. Thank you. You're a miracle worker."

"I'll do your hair like this for the wedding, I think. Mum, is there anyone in your family we could invite to the wedding? Yossi has no-one coming. You must have someone here. What about your Dad?"

"You and Yossi are all I need. We're late. Clean your teeth. And have you got clean PE gear for tomorrow?"

As they wait to get onto the motorway at Gillies Avenue Yossi says to her, "Claire, I can't believe they dragged all that up when it has nothing to do with the Peterus. It must have been hard to watch."

She pats him on the arm and gives him a half smile. He has the Chopin *Piano Trio* playing that they both love.

"We haven't heard this for ages," she says.

"How was the dress? Roi said I'm not to look at it until the day," Yossi says.

"God, they're old-fashioned, this young lot. Weddings are huge again."

She turns the music down.

"Yoss, I always had to be the mother, when I was a child. I had to be the calm, sensible one. I just want Roimata to get a chance to be a kid. All this chaos I'm in at work – her helping choose my dress – she's not having to mother me is she?"

"Darling, she loves planning how you will look. You never give a toss about your clothes. She's excited about the wedding. She's happy."

Claire's cellphone rings as they walk from the car to the restaurant. She needs to answer. Rory Peteru could be found at any time.

"Claire Bowerman."

"Hi, Claire. My name's Simon Flaxstone. I'm researching a book about the disappearance of Kathryn Phillips. I saw you on the news."

She says nothing.

"Claire, I believe your father was innocent. I have some alternative theories about what may have happened to her."

Yeah, sure. She's heard it all before.

"I don't wish to talk to the media." She hangs up.

It's started.

17

YOSSI

The restaurant is elegant and understated. Miles Davis' cool trumpet billows and swoops. Mostly doctors, the men talk about cricket. Yossi has nothing to say, drinks his smooth pinot noir. Claire looks striking in the flickering candlelight. While she talks, she moves her hands for emphasis, which makes her collarbones dance close to the surface and stretch her skin taut. Yossi loves seeing her with her hair down like this. He cannot stop admiring the sweep and shine of it.

Men and women at other tables look at her too but Claire doesn't show any sign of noticing. The women are talking about the Peteru case. Claire listens attentively to all their arguments. She speaks just twice, both times to say the same thing.

"He will die without this surgery."

Yossi's tortellini is glorious. He must start using truffle oil. It's earthy and fills his senses. People talk less now, apart from saying how delicious their food is. When their plates are cleared, Claire excuses herself. The heavyset woman seated opposite him speaks to Janet.

"I've always meant to ask you. Is Claire related to Patrick Bowerman?"

Janet nods, then she firmly changes the subject.

Later, Janet confides in him, speaking quietly, the room full of loud chatter. "I'm sorry about Rosie being tactless. I'll tell her Claire doesn't want to talk about her father."

"Why do some people have such a strong memory of it?" he asks.

"I think it's the fact the police might have lied. My mum said the whole of New Zealand was shocked at that. My dad was a cop."

"The police might have lied? What do you mean?"

"At one of the trials, a young policeman testified that Claire told him her father had confessed to the murder. Claire denied it in court. The final judge ruled that Claire's mother and the policeman had concocted the story together to implicate Claire's father. She was young, Yossi. It must have been horrible for her."

Janet's fiddling with the candle, pressing on the molten wax, making it slump a little. Loud bursts of laughter and cutlery scraping on plates force him to lean in and speak close to Janet's ear.

"Did your father think Patrick was guilty?"

"Yes, but he thought they'd never proved it. Most people believed he was guilty. I'm afraid he is rather a despised character. Poor Claire."

Yossi is beginning to understand his darling Claire's passion for facts. Gossip, innuendo, guessing, opinion, belief; all must have swirled around her throughout her life. Has there been anything his Claire can trust?

Me, Claire. Marry me. You can trust me.

18

YOSSI

Sunday morning when he wakes at Waiheke, Claire is asleep beside him. She looks so peaceful. The first thing he thinks about is Roimata and her birth father. It's urgent that they tell her. Claire is putting it off. He has thought about it and he is fine with it. It's just part of life.

There's a knock on the door and it's Roi, carrying Vogel's toast topped with thinly sliced tomato, and plunger coffee.

"Wow, Roi, thank you. Yum," Claire says, waking up, covering herself with the light blue summer blanket and pulling on a t-shirt all in one movement. She reaches up and pulls her daughter down to kiss her.

"How come you're up?" Yossi asks.

Roimata usually sleeps in until late morning these days, which drives her mother crazy.

"Charlotte and I are going wind-surfing. She's got a new board. The wind's perfect now."

Yossi sees Claire tense, sit up and look through the bi-fold doors at the sky. She is always nervous when Roi is in the water.

"It's beautiful," he says. "There's hardly any wind. They'll be fine."

"Where are you going from? Have you looked at the forecast?" Claire asks Roi.

"I guess just down here in Ruby Bay. From our jetty."

"Make sure you take lifejackets. We have a spare one if Charlie needs one."

"Mum, I'm not a baby."

Claire looks at Yossi. He shrugs, knowing they have to let Roimata go.

"Roi," he says. "Can you refill my cup? Please?"

"Ok." She bounces out.

"She's in a good mood for a morning," says Claire. "Long may it last." She runs her fingers through her hair, trying to tidy it.

"Claire, listen," Yossi whispers. "It's a good time now. We need to tell her."

"What? No. No."

Her tone of voice makes him wince. She's overreacting.

"We're all together and happy. We're not rushing. You work such long hours during the week."

"No. We haven't planned it. I don't know what I'm going to say. No, Yossi. I don't know how to tell her this, it's a big deal," says Claire.

"How to tell who what?" Roi says, putting the coffee plunger down on Yossi's bedside table then climbing over him and squirming down in between the two of them, holding a piece of toast between her teeth. Yossi can smell her freshly shampooed hair and he takes her warm hand, which squeezes his.

"Nothing," says Claire.

Roi snuggles down, crunching toast in his ear. It's the right time. Claire will never be ready.

"Roimata, your real father, I mean your birth father –" says Yossi. God, it's awkward.

Roi sits bolt upright, bumping the headboard against the wall. "What?"

Yossi looks to Claire, who glares at him and puts her arm around Roimata. He'll just have to ignore her. Once it's out, it's out.

"Darling, your birth father, well, his sister, has contacted me," Claire says.

"Who is he? Who is he?"

"His name is Brent Te Hira."

"Why haven't you told me his name before?"

"I told you, he was married. I was worried about hurting his wife and family."

"Brent. Brent." Roi gets out of bed, clambering over Yossi. She dances around the room. "God. My father. Brent. Brent," she sings. "Where is he? Have you talked to him? Can I meet him?"

Claire looks pale and overwhelmed. Yossi moves over and puts his arm around her. She shrugs him off, wraps her arm around her knees, puts her head in her hands.

"Slow down, Roi," Yossi says. "Your mum met his sister – Rachel – through work. She wants to meet you."

"When can I meet him?"

Yossi says, "He lives in Germany. You need time to think about this. You can meet his sister if you want to. Think about it though." The girl is whirling around. She's forgotten about the toast she's holding and a piece of tomato flops onto the floor.

"Yes, yes. What does he look like? What did he say about having me?"

Yossi stands up, grabs her and holds her.

"Mum?" She holds out an arm.

Claire gets out of bed and leans against Roi too until the three of them are hugging.

"I love you my darling. We'll work all this out. You don't have to do anything you don't want to," Claire says.

"I can't wait to meet him," Roi says.

Yossi looks at Claire's face over Roi's head. He smiles at her. She looks away. There's a loud buzz from Roi's phone.

"Charlotte's going to be down on the jetty in ten minutes." Roimata skips to the door, tickling Yossi on her way past. She starts to go out the door, and then comes back.

"Mum, Mum. I want to meet him soon. Please."

Claire has turned away from him. He goes to hug her. She stiffens. Starts pulling on a sweatshirt.

"I'm going to sit on the jetty and watch them. Make sure they wear their life jackets. It's dangerous out there."

God, he gets tired of her negativity.

19

On Monday, up on the lime green surgical ward, the sickest child is three-year-old Triumph.

"Hi, I'm Claire. I'm one of the surgeons here. I'm sorry, I know you've met heaps of us but Triumph has complicated problems and we all specialise in different bits."

"Hi."

"Sorry – your name is?"

"Patch."

Mum's voice is deep and raspy, the shy smile revealing missing top teeth in a generous mouth with blue-black lips. The shapeless red jersey, pilled and covered in lint, and her black woollen hat lend her a comical look. She fidgets with her son, licking her delicate fingers and shaping his fringe into a quiff, picking fluff off his clothes, giving him frequent sips of water from the glass on his bedside table.

"Did he have a settled night?" Claire asks her.

"Yeah."

"Did you get any sleep?"

"Mm."

"I'm the one that will actually operate on Triumph. I'm going to try to fix the blockage in his bowel that's giving him so much pain. Here's a drawing of the bowel and intestines. I'll show you what I'm going to do."

Patch's head goes down. Claire tries hard, making eye contact, reassuring, making jokes.

"You just do what you want, Doctor."

Should she even be trying to explain? Patch nods and smiles at everything Claire says. She fusses over the boy all the time, stroking him, straightening his blanket.

Crude tattoos scar her skin, a blue cross so close to her right eye that Claire cannot help envisioning, with horror, the scene of its execution. A spider's web gloves her left hand up to the knuckles, above which float four spindly letters: L O V E. A wobbly swastika decorates the underside of her right arm.

A man comes to the doorway of the room, sees Claire beside Triumph's bed, scowls, turns his back and waits. The other mothers look at each other with slightly raised eyebrows. He's a stocky bulldozer of a man, wearing a Mongrel Mob leather jacket. The slavering bulldog emblazoned on his back is causing a frisson throughout the ward.

Patch looks at him and giggles.

"That's the father."

"He's welcome to come in. I can go through it again for him."

"Oh nah! He's too shy."

"Go on. I'd like to meet him. He should be in on this."

Patch grins and uses her eyebrows and head to try to summon the man. But he ignores her.

"Hi. I'm Claire. I'll be doing the surgery on your son." Claire moves over to the doorway, smiling and holding out her hand, which is ignored.

She has to avert her eyes from the tattoo on his neck, a dotted line with the legend CUT HERE right on top of his Adam's apple. It makes her slightly queasy. He squirms a few times and hardly acknowledges she's spoken to him. He doesn't make eye contact. Patch comes to stand beside her.

"Knockers, get that patch off when you talk to the doctor."

He takes off his sleeveless leather jacket, turns it inside out, and puts it on again. They go off outside for a cigarette.

20

CLAIRE'S DREADING THE DINNER PARTY. When she ventures into the kitchen after work the smells are glorious. Garlic, lemon zest, roasted nuts. In the oven, cherry tomatoes shrivel and burst, spilling sticky seeds down their sides. On the chopping board behind the sink, neat piles of pungent herbs: basil, parsley and feathery coriander. Yossi's going all out. Roimata's into it too. Yossi's teaching her to make the tiny almond crescents he calls *rugelach*. As the two of them dust the cookies with billows of icing sugar, the powdery residue lands on their eyebrows, elbows, ears.

Itzhak Perlman playing klezmer fills the house, at once exuberant and doleful. Their favourite cooking music. Claire longs for London, when Yossi would listen to this while he cooked for his sharp, argumentative Israeli friends. Claire had loved their opinionated discussions. She'd felt exotic, clever, alive.

Yossi and Roimata dance around the kitchen, each trying to out-silly the other. Claire wishes they weren't going to so much trouble. She doesn't know yet what she wants to do about Rachel, what her role will be in their lives.

"Can I help?" Claire asks.

"No, no," says Yossi. "You've been working. Enjoy yourself! Relax."

Enjoy herself? She can't seem to focus on anything. There's always work she could do, notes to finish up, journals to read, and reports to write. However, none of it's urgent. She checks the bathroom is clean, but Yossi has the place spotless.

Perhaps she needs sunshine. It usually helps. With an hour to go, Claire sits out in the last of the evening sun with the morning newspaper. She hasn't had time all day to read it, but finds no interest in any of the stories. Shark sightings, boating accidents, the Prime Minister holidaying in Hawaii. She listens to the birds with her eyes closed. What does Rachel want from them? How much does she remember of Claire's past? Has she even realised who Claire is? What will she tell Roimata?

It's time to get showered and dressed ready for their guest. She can do this.

"Oh – I'm sorry but –" Rachel is weepy just moments after Roi answers the door.

Claire offers to take her coat but Rachel's too busy staring at Roimata. Tears streaming, she takes Roi by the shoulders, staring at her, leaning in and giving her a long hug.

"You have your father's nose."

Claire wants to push them apart. "Rachel, this is Yossi, Roimata's father." A bit pointed but she needs to make it clear right from the start.

"Tēnā koe," Rachel says as she kisses Roimata on both cheeks, saying "Mmm", tears streaming. "I have presents."

Rachel reaches into her basket. She hands Claire a bottle of designer-looking olive oil. For Yossi, a book on Māori music. He looks delighted. They've been talking on the phone, then. She kisses Yossi too and then Yossi disappears to the kitchen. Roi's present is a framed photo of Brent. Goodness she moves fast.

Rachel's carrying photo albums under her arm and Roi questions her as soon as they're seated.

"Have you brought more photos of my – of Brent?"

"Let the poor woman have a drink and something to eat first," says Claire.

Rachel pats the seat beside her on the couch and Roimata obeys and sits beside her.

"There he is. This is about the time your Mum met him." She turns the photo over. "Yeah, Italy 1994, Siemens Social Team."

"You chose good genes for me, Mum."

That's a bit flippant. He was married. It's something to be

ashamed of, not joked about. How it would have broken his wife's heart had she known. She's glad Yossi's in the kitchen and can't hear.

"Here's Brent's family."

Claire sits on the couch opposite. Roi hands over each photo to her when she's finished. So that's the wife. An angular, laughing face, fair hair, bright floral dress. She looks quite a lot like a young Claire. Shit. His two daughters look a lot like Roi too. Long forgotten guilt swamps Claire. How could she have?

"Marta and Maddy speak German of course, but they're good at English too. Their Māori is bad. It's a crack-up hearing these two brown nieces of mine speaking German. Always takes a while to get used to. It's going to take a while to get used to your accent too, you Londoner," she jokes to Roi.

"I hope you like Israeli food," says Yossi, motioning to them all to be seated at the table. Hummus made from scratch, fava bean spread, falafel, grilled chicken, homemade pita bread, the best garlic sauce in the world.

"It all looks delicious. Thank you."

"Claire, would you like some of this wine Rachel brought? It looks lovely."

"Can't, sorry. I'm on call tonight."

"I'll have a sip," Roimata says.

"No," Yossi and Claire say in unison.

Roimata laughs.

"Shall I say grace?" says Rachel.

Now what are they going to do?

"Sure," says Yossi. Neither Claire nor Yossi incline their heads, but Roimata does.

When the delicate *rugelach* arrive with a sweet sticky wine, Rachel says to Yossi, "This is so yummy. Can you adopt me?" Everyone else laughs at her joke. Claire watches Roimata carefully, but Roi seems fine. Sailing through. Claire wants to talk to her, to comfort her, but this cool, confident girl seems unapproachable.

"Claire, I saw on television you're involved with that boy with cancer, the one where Mum and Dad don't want treatment," Rachel says.

Here we go. Another lecture. No doubt we're being paternalistic. Based on what she's seen on television. Great. Claire braces herself. She can't talk about it anyway. It's confidential. Why don't people get that?

"Gosh that must be hard. Of course that boy needs surgery. You're doing the right thing, Claire. Roimata, you have a very brave mother. And amazingly successful."

Claire plays Rachel's speech back in her head. Amazingly successful. Yeah right. Doesn't she mean, it's amazing you're a doctor, coming from that family?

"It's great having family here," Yossi says to Roi as they see Rachel out. "That was so much fun."

Can't he see the danger?

21

IT'S 1:30AM. JUST AS WELL she didn't drink at dinner. Trying to wake herself by winding down the windows, Claire seems to get every red light on her way to the hospital, even though the streets are empty. She winds the windows up again when she sees a homeless man drifting along Park Road towards the Domain and then chides herself for being nervous of some poor vagrant she could probably push over. The man lifts his arms and crosses them, protecting himself, as if under attack, from a loud thudding and a high whine overhead. It takes Claire a moment to see the red lights of the Westpac rescue helicopter swoop low and disappear behind the tall hospital building. That will be her patients. Victims of a serious road accident up north. One adult fatality and three seriously smashed-up children for Starship. Why three young children are even out in a car after midnight, no-one's told her. It's not her job to ask. It's all hands on deck.

While she parks her car and walks carefully across the uneven asphalt to the Children's Emergency Entrance she steels herself. Accidents at this time of night usually involve alcohol. Facing relatives can be horrible. According to the paramedics attending the crash, the baby she will work on is young and seriously hurt.

But the Charge Nurse tells her that her baby's on the next helicopter and it could be a while. Not a good sign. She heads to the mock-rainforest atrium, picks her way through the fake log seats that are like an obstacle course in the dim lighting. The recorded chirping of birds, someone's idea of a soothing sound, is unsettling at night. She glides in the yellow lift up to the hushed, semi-dark ward to check on her other charges.

Triumph lies on his side, sucking his thumb, fast asleep.

In the bed opposite Che McKenzie is awake. He's whimpering. A dark shape by the bed holds him and Claire, as her eyes adjust, sees it is Patch, Triumph's mum.

"Hi, is he ok? It's Claire Bowerman."

"Oh hi. Yeah. Sorry. He had a nightmare. No-one's ever here with him. I felt sorry for him. I know it's not my business."

"I'll get him a hot chocolate. Would you like a cup of tea?"

A few sips and some cuddles lull Che back to sleep. He looks cherubic, long, wet eyelashes resting on downy skin. Patch and Claire sip their hot drinks and speak softly in the semi-darkness. Patch's voice is rough, the result of too many cigarettes and, Claire has no doubt, a life with too much struggle.

"I feel so sorry for this kid," says Patch.

Claire has to be careful what she says. She can't talk about one patient to another.

"Have you talked to his mother?"

"She's hardly ever here. She's got some horrible man," she giggles. "I'm terrible, I just want to take them all home with me. There are others here too. I want to adopt them all."

"How many have you got?" Claire asks her.

"Just Triumph now. And we've got another boy, not mine, he belongs to Knockers. He's fifteen."

Claire is glad her face can't be seen. Knockers only looks in his twenties himself.

"How long have you looked after him?"

"His mother left him with us when he was eight. She didn't want him any more. We never see her. Knockers didn't know about him. He was just a kid. Pedro's a good boy. Helps with Triumph."

"Has he joined the gang?"

"No. We're not going to let him. Knockers would give him a hiding if he showed any sign." Patch leans over and strokes Che, who's stirred a bit. He mutters and settles.

"My other boy died."

Oh God. Like any parent, Claire shudders to hear of a child's death.

"What happened?"

"He lived with my Nana. Down Porirua. Got meningitis. Some of these kids though, like Che. No-one wants them. Arseholes of men looking after them. Whoops, sorry."

It's hushed and dark on the ward. In the dimness, Claire stares at Che. She's almost forgotten Patch is there when the husky voice says, "Best thing I can say about my childhood is, I survived it. Hope he survives his."

They sip their tea.

"You're pregnant again? Is this one going well?" Claire asks her.

"Oh yeah. I can't wait. But I want to get Triumph better first, before this baby arrives to worry about."

Claire's pager buzzes as she and Patch hear the roar of the helicopter landing on the helipad below the window. She heads downstairs, where they tell her the baby did not survive the flight. She looks at the paper work. Violet Eliza McDonald. What a beautiful name. Six months. Deceased. Her heart lurches.

She hurries to theatre to help with the sicker of the other two children.

After rounds that afternoon Claire sits down with Patch. Triumph is a bit flushed and grizzly.

"It's probably ok, just a small setback," Claire tells her.

The nurses are letting Patch do more for her son. Claire watches her sponge his face deftly.

"How prem was he?"

"Twenty-four weeker."

"As teeny as they get."

"He's a fighter."

Claire considers mentioning that pregnant Patch should not be smoking. But she resists. She doesn't want to risk her relationship with Patch. Patch is a good mother. She won't stop smoking just because Claire points out something she already knows; no doubt it's one of few comforts in her life. On balance, it's better to just support her. Many of her colleagues would disagree, of course, especially those likely to end up treating an underweight, fragile baby in NICU.

In the bed across from them, the little assault victim, Che, is playing on a Game Boy that Claire's given him, an old one of Roi's. He looks up in pleasure when his mother's voice booms out at the ward office outside. Everyone can hear her.

"Yes, I'm allowed to see him."

Claire notices Che look down at the game in panic. She goes over.

"I can look after your game for you if you like. I promise I'll give it back when Mum's gone."

He hands it to her just in time as Heaven makes her entrance.

"My baaaaay beeeeee," she shouts theatrically and hurries to his side.

Claire sees his face. Sometimes they love their useless parents so much it could break your heart.

Heaven squashes Che's face to her chest. The colourful curtains make a ripping sound as she pulls them around his bed.

Ten minutes later, when Claire returns, she peers through the curtain. Heaven slumps in a chair facing away from her son, reading a trashy magazine. Che lies on his bed, staring at the wall.

There's a note on the table, with a phone number, in Yossi's elegant writing.

Ring Simon Flaxstone. Writing book about your father.

Yossi comes into the kitchen.

"Tough night?"

She crumples the note and throws it in the bin.

Yossi goes to grab it.

"Did you get that message? It's great news, Claire. He sounded an interesting guy. Wants to talk to you about your father."

"Well I don't want to talk to him. I've told him that."

"It's ok, Claire, he's crusading for your father. He believes your father's innocent. It's exciting." He grabs her from behind, semi-dancing with her. "Wouldn't it be great to know your father was not a bad man?"

She doesn't answer. Moves out of his embrace. She heads upstairs, calling over her shoulder. "If he rings again, tell him I want nothing to do with him."

Yossi assumes her father is innocent. It's lovely that he's an optimist but sometimes it's hard to live with someone so unrealistic. She has to be the realist. Or pessimist, as Yossi would call it.

She hears the phone ring half an hour later but leaves it to the others as she writes up notes. Roimata calls upstairs.

"Mum, it's Simon Flaxstone. About your Dad."

"I don't wish to speak to him."

She hears Roimata take down his phone number again. Why can't they just leave this alone?

"Mum," Roimata calls up. "You should talk to him. I talked to him the other day. He says your father's innocent."

"What? You're not to talk to him. What did you say?"

"But he's on your side."

"Dinner's ready," Yossi shouts.

Claire stops and rubs her neck. Her eyelids feel heavy and she's irritated with Roimata. But she catches herself. It's not Roimata or Yossi's fault. They don't understand her weird family. Nor does she. She just does what she needs to in order to survive.

Downstairs the kitchen's suffused with warmth and a rich herby smell that makes her limbs sluggish. With a flourish, Yossi puts a sizzling dish on the table.

"Sautéed beef with white wine and rosemary," he announces.

"Mum, why won't you talk to that guy? Granddad might be innocent."

"Roimata. My father was in and out of prison and there was a lot of media attention. I don't trust journalists. I'm sorry. I have moved on. There's no point in dragging it all up."

"And what about me? I'd like to know. I'd like to meet my grandfather."

"You're already finding out about your birth father. Isn't that enough for the moment?"

"Why do you have to say it like that?"

"Like what?"

"Like it's beneath you, or it's trouble or something."

"Roimata –"

"You're the one that's taught me that no-one's evil. You're all understanding when it comes to your patients but not your family, no. You're a hypocrite."

A car toots outside. Roi grabs her bag and starts to go.

"Roimata. Who's that? Where are you going?"

"It's Aunty Rachel. I'm going around there."

Claire looks at Yossi, who looks as surprised as her.

"But your father's cooked this beautiful dinner. It's a school night. You didn't ask."

"I did so. I told Yossi yesterday. God!"

She stalks out.

"Did she ask?"

"I'd forgotten but, yes, she did tell me actually."

"She should stay in on school nights."

"I think Rachel's actually helping her with a school project or something. I think it's Māori history."

"I've never seen her like that. What's her problem?"

"There's no problem. She's a teenager."

Roimata arrives home a couple of hours later, gripping several photo albums, a new greenstone fishhook on a cord around her neck. She tells them Rachel's asked them to come that weekend to a family reunion at her marae in the Bay of Plenty.

"That would be fantastic," Yossi says, before Claire has a chance to say anything. Great. Now she's going to be even more the bad guy if she objects.

"Wow. This is going to be so cool," says Roimata. "Mum, Rachel's teaching me a song."

"Don't you think it could wait until another time?" Claire says to Yossi later. "We've got lots of planning to do for the wedding."

"I'm looking forward to it. My first marae experience. It'll be great for us all to get away down south."

She knows he is right.

"This is huge for her," she says.

22

When Claire gets to work early, the first thing she does is check on Triumph. He's lethargic. Her gut's telling her that something's not quite right. She orders more tests. Janet beckons her into the corridor.

"Have you seen the paper?" she asks.

"No, not yet," Claire says.

"The Peterus –"

"God, don't tell me. He's had a miracle cure now."

"Yeah of course. But Claire, there's also stuff about you."

Janet hands it to her.

On the front page a TV celebrity holds Rory on his knee while pointing a microphone at Kate Peteru. Bold headlines declare: *Mother begs hospital – just give him a scan and see.* She skims the article, aware she's due in surgery. The alternative practitioner and Rory's parents believe his tumour has shrunk but can't get anyone to scan it as long as they are in hiding. Yeah right. A week or two of snake oil treatment.

You won't believe how they stick together. It's a real old boys club, says the celebrity. *Every time we tried to take him for a scan, they wanted to dob in the family. One clinic finally did it for us secretly.*

What? Dob them in? They are wanted by the police. Why are people taking this so lightly?

The article finishes by saying that the results of the scan will be revealed on the TV show tonight. Claire's pager goes off and she gets a text at the same time. They're waiting for her in pre-op where she has a long list this morning. The CEO wants to talk to her. Probably about this article. Later. Surgery comes first.

First up, a simple tongue-tie. The mother's hysterical. No way she's going to let this one be with her child while he's put under. The registrar had met them last night to get the forms signed and she'd done all the reassuring she could but apparently the mother is making a meal of it. The only thing to do is just get on with it. She says "Hi" to the mother and then "Off we go" to the child and she and the orderly start pushing the trolley away.

Just as they move, a TV crew comes into the room.

"What are you doing here? Do you have permission?" the theatre nurse says.

The reporter just smiles and motions at the guy with the camera to film the mother, who's sobbing to Claire. "Please, please look after my baby. Please don't hurt him. Please let him be safe."

Claire steps in between the bed they are pushing and the camera.

"Get out of here. Someone call Security."

The mother's wailing as they push the boy through the doors into theatre. The cameraman chases them, as though to come through too.

"This is an operating theatre! It's sterile. Get out!" Claire says as she shuts the door in the man's face.

She makes it home just in time to see the show. She sends Roimata upstairs to do homework and then sits down on the squashy linen couch. Yossi lies beside her, his head in her lap. As the martial opening music blares he says, "Claire-Bear, I saw a promo earlier during the News. I don't think it's going to be good."

The item starts with footage from the morning. It's put together so that it looks as though Claire's angry slamming of the door to theatre is dismissing the patient's mother, who can be seen sobbing and begging her not to hurt her son.

"That was the film crew I was shutting out," she says to Yossi.

The programme cuts to the corridor outside pre-op with the nurse trying her best to evict them and the mother happily talking to the reporter. *It just makes you wonder if you can trust her, you know. It's very frightening really.*

Grainy black and white footage wavers on the screen. Police

bundle a young girl into a car and drive away, the girl's face pale and solemn in the back seat. It takes Claire a second to realise it's her, aged nine. She'd called 111 when her mother had harmed herself. Which time was that? Wrists. Scratched only. Not a very serious attempt she realises now. She'd cleaned up her mother's mess while she'd waited for the police to arrive. Put on a load of washing.

Yossi sits up straight and throws a cushion at the television. He puts his arm around Claire. "You should complain," he says. "It's bloody ridiculous."

"Shh," she says. "They're still talking about Rory."

The CEO of Starship does a good job staying calm and not sounding defensive.

I can't talk about individual cases. If my doctors advise me someone needs treatment then it is them I listen to."

Good on her. Go Meryl.

But she's clearly unprepared for the questions about Claire's family.

Is it true that the surgeon's father was the convicted murderer Patrick Bowerman, later pardoned?

What? What on earth has this to do with this Peteru case?

Isn't it arrogant of her to force treatment on this child against the wishes of his parents?

This is a hospital decision. Miss Bowerman is simply the surgeon who will carry out the operation. She's not even in charge of the case. Now leave my hospital please.

What right do doctors have to decide they know better than parents?

Please leave.

The story finishes on Rory having a scan, the reporter holding Kate Peteru's hand. *The tumour's quite small now*, says the reporter's voice. *Kate and Isa'ako believe it's shrunk.*

Claire tries to see the films. Yes, it's small at the moment. That's the chemo, people.

But, unbelievably, we at TVNZ cannot get the information from Starship about the size of the tumour before the alternative treatment in order to compare. They refuse to talk to us and the Peterus are understandably too afraid to contact the hospital.

Of course a bloody TV show can't be told. It's private and confidential information. Claire turns at a noise. It's Roimata in the doorway. How long's she been there?

"Why didn't you tell me it was on?"

"I didn't want you to see it. It's not important Roi. Just a silly media beat-up."

"Don't patronise me. You treat me like a baby. Is that boy going to be all right? Why don't they find him? Why do those people hate you?"

Claire reaches for Roi and goes to pull her down on her knee. Wants to bury her face in the beautiful hair. But Roimata shakes her off.

"Is he going to be all right?" she asks again.

"We'll find him," Claire says. "He'll be fine." And then kicks herself. She knows better than to make promises to children.

23

THE BAY OF PLENTY, 2010

They wait outside the marae. The entrance reminds Claire of a child's drawing of a house; two beams slope up from the top of the gate to form the roof. Along the beams, carved human-like figures curl and grimace, their eyes made of translucent pāua shell. A low brown fence runs from either side of the gate encircling a few low buildings and a worn paved area.

People arrive in small groups. Rachel, smart as always, stands out in her black trousers and long red cardigan. A greenstone pendant lends her tremendous *gravitas*. Claire watches Rachel greet people with kisses, and introduce Roimata, who is exclaimed over, and kissed repeatedly. She looks people in the eye and kisses them right back. Claire would hate to be the centre of attention like this, to be faced with so much that is new, but Roimata is clearly enjoying it, laughing when teased about her accent.

It's a little chilly in the shade. She'd been unsure what to wear, has chosen a floral dress. Every time she's ever visited a marae she has loved it, but today she's more than just a curious visitor. There is so much she is ignorant about. She would hate to give offence.

A woman with elegant grey curls comes over to her. "We'll be right here beside you all the way, guiding you, so you have nothing to worry about, darling," she says, as if she can read Claire's thoughts.

Rachel brings over a shy young woman with a baby in a sling. It's Eli Tipene and his mother. Claire has a cuddle. He's gorgeous. He's thriving. Claire lifts his little t-shirt and checks his scar. It's perfect. She blows a raspberry on his tummy and he chuckles.

"I knew you'd do a great job," she tells the young girl.

All at once it starts. Rachel gathers them up and takes them towards the gate, one hand on Roimata's arm as a woman's voice begins keening. *Haere mai … Haere mai … … Haere mai ki te whānau … …* The sound is gravelly, cracked, painful.

Rachel steers them behind the men, making sure they stick to the slow, respectful pace. They move in a huddle, their heads slightly bowed.

The voice grows louder, wavers, and dies away as it slides down in pitch. *Haere mai.* The woman's hands tremble. Claire hasn't heard it for years and she's forgotten the power of the karanga. Her nerves tingle and her eyes sting. She mustn't cry. Yet there is something about this sound that could get her weeping, from somewhere deep inside. A woman from her side replies, her voice much deeper, equally beautiful.

Through the gate the low, plain meeting-house. There are benches laid out for them, the people of this marae will sit in front of their wharenui, facing the visitors. A few people are already seated, some with their eyes closed, some staring at Roimata. There are whispers and gasps.

Claire hears Rachel whisper to Roi, "Don't worry, darling, they're just noticing how much you look like your father and your grandmother."

Roimata blushes but she smiles.

The haka begins. A group of mostly young men, some of them shy and a little awkward a moment ago, are now stamping their feet and shouting, in unison. The engagement and intensity are awe-inspiring. Now Claire cannot stop her tears. Yossi and Roimata both widen their eyes with pleasure and amazement.

One of the young men advances towards them, hyper-alert, glaring. He places a sprig of greenery on the ground a short distance from the older men at the front of her group, and backs away. A middle-aged man leans down and picks it up.

"We've been challenged and we have responded. It is now a

place of safety, of mutual respect," Rachel says to her quietly. "Now we will have the formal speeches."

A man takes Yossi's arm and leads him to the front bench to sit with the men, while Rachel leads Claire and Roimata to the one behind. She used to think this was sexist. It's complicated, Rachel had told Roimata last night. Right now Claire's just relieved to let Yossi take the limelight. She feels grateful for his protecting her. They sit, everyone taking their time. Then an old man in the front row opposite coughs loudly several times as he slowly gets to his feet. This has an electric effect as everyone stops shuffling and moving. He has a stiff leg and carries an elaborately carved walking stick.

Tēnā koutou. Rachel whispers a translation into Claire's ear.

… He's welcoming all the guests to this beautiful marae on this beautiful day, especially you and Roimata. He is telling everyone that Roimata was born on the other side of the world in London and that she has found her way here to us. Inside the sacred house, she will find many photos of her grandmother Roimata. When she was young, Roimata was beautiful and broke many hearts, just as your Roimata will do today.

Rachel is leaning in close to her, so that she can whisper the translation, her hand squeezing Claire's hand. She is so lucky that Rachel, is so warm, so strong. But what about Roimata? She looks smiling and attentive. She has her own translator, a young woman with an eyebrow ring and half of her head shaved. This is so big for Roi, but it's territory where Claire cannot help her.

He's telling us of his joy that our whānau has reclaimed Roimata and that the blood of her father and grandparents and all his ancestors flows in her veins. Roimata was born across the ocean, but this is her tūrangawaewae, her place to stand in the world … and the heart of the ancestors beats here…

When his song is sung, Rachel leans over and touches Yossi, who stands up. Rachel had trained him up last night in their motel. Being a man, he should speak if he is willing, and he is allowed to speak in English. So Claire had gone and had a bath, while he'd struggled to learn a bit of a greeting.

"Tēnā koutou, tēnā koutou, tēnā koutou katoa. My name's Yosef Shalev but everyone calls me Yossi. First, thank you so much for your welcome to this sacred and spiritual place. Being here with you reminds me of my homeland Israel, especially the humour, and the warmth towards guests. It is fantastic for me to begin to understand the blood that flows in Roimata's veins. As you know, I am not her biological father but she came into my life when she was little, and she has given me nothing but light and joy ever since. And this she will bring to you too, I can see that.

I am sorry I cannot speak your elegant language but I would like you to indulge me while I sing you a song in my first language, Hebrew. It is a lullaby and I am singing ...

Sleep child sleep
this is a war of generations
the tears have dried already for a long time."

He sings. The kaumātua leans on his stick and listens intently to the plaintive melody. He smiles, delighted with what he's hearing.

Rachel stands beside Yossi, humming along as she picks up the melody. She takes his arm and they both return to their places.

Rachel continues to translate for her as the locals and then the visitors speak. Many of the speeches are about the meeting house, explaining to Roimata how the house reflects her ancestry and her stories. Her grandfather's bravery in going to war at seventeen is mentioned in one speech, too. Māoridom lost so many young men in that war, so many fathers and potential leaders, Claire's father had always said. A whole generation short on fathers.

When the formal speeches and songs are over, the old man who spoke first stands and speaks again, this time in English.

"I am enjoying the knowledge that our precious treasure, our lost Roimata, has been in safe hands, the hands of a good man. And a good woman." He looks at Claire. "I understand, Dr Bowerman, that you are a healer and have already helped our whānau before we knew about Roimata. Thank you and welcome." Then back to Roimata. "Roimata, you are home. Once again, welcome precious Roimata. Your name means tears. There will be many tears shed in memory of your great-grandmother today. And tears of joy that you are here with us."

Five or six women in track pants and hooded sweatshirts make their way up and join the speaker as he starts singing. They harmonise effortlessly. Claire's eyes fill again. She looks at Roimata, who is watching intently, nodding her head to the music.

"Ok," says Pereme, as it ends. "Now let's have a cup of tea and a smoke …"

Claire stands up because everyone else does. She fumbles in her bag for a tissue, forcing her lips to smile at the people who catch her eye.

Rachel brings a slight, elderly woman over to Claire. She is wiping her glasses with a hanky.

"Tears of joy," she explains in a high, cracked voice. She stretches up and presses Claire to her nose again, murmuring, her hands shaking. Claire feels tears prickle again, the warmth of this tiny woman enveloping her.

"My darling. This is so right. I have a story to tell you. See the photo over there?"

In pride of place, a photo of Nanny Roimata stands on an easel. A feather cloak has been placed around the photo. Claire nods.

"Nanny Roimata."

"Last night, we had a meeting here. We talked of precious things, of your Roimata and the way she can claim her link to our whānau. I remember her grandmother well." The woman clasps Claire's hand tight with bony hands, her eyes bright. She speaks softly, reverently. "When we were finished and we got up, I looked at the photo and it was crying! There were tears running down the face. We all knew this was a sign from our kuia. This hui is tikanga. We're doing the right thing."

Now what was she going to say? This is so far out of her comfort zone.

Before she knows it she's in the kitchen peeling potatoes. She doesn't want to do the wrong thing. She doesn't even know where Roimata is.

Driving back to Auckland, Yossi can't stop talking, raving about the experience, and how great it was going to be for Roimata.

They've left her there with Rachel for another night. "They're so spiritual," he says. "I didn't expect them to be so religious."

"I know. They have totally embraced a colonising, Pākehā god," she laughs.

"Oh, yes," he says. "I didn't think about that."

"It's her heritage and you have done the right thing in bringing her to it," Yossi says.

Is it her heritage? Is Roimata Māori because of her blood, her DNA? Brent has not been her father in any other way.

"What is it?" Yossi asks.

"What?"

"You seem so uncomfortable with all this. Are you worried she will have all these new people, and it will take her away from you?"

"Of course I am," says Claire. "But there's more to it than that."

"What then?"

"Look, I really love so many aspects of the culture. But there are problems. Deep-seated problems, ok?"

Yossi says nothing as he negotiates a hazardous bend. He's finding the back roads in New Zealand rough. Claire wonders for a minute why she isn't driving.

"You'll need to slow down. Those signs mean curvy corners up ahead."

"I know what the signs mean," says Yossi.

The wheels on Claire's side of the car veer onto the gravel shoulder with a loud spurt of stones. They hit a hairpin bend, travelling downhill. Claire is quiet as Yossi grips the wheel and creeps around the corner.

"Look, as well as poverty, the problems I'm talking about are caused by racism and colonisation. I know that. Oh, I don't know what I'm trying to say."

The only thing Claire knows for sure is that she has succeeded because she pushed it all down, because she ran away, because she rescued herself. Love means dangerous vulnerability. The bloody past, the way it weighs down on the present.

"I'm just a bit of a loner. Not used to being part of something bigger like this."

"Is your concern," says Yossi, "that you think she may fall into bad company? This is our Roi. You have, *we* have," he corrects himself, "already given her good values."

"There are a lot of damaged people. I am worried about all sorts of things. Whether it will distract Roi. Whether there will be demands on her."

Claire feels tears coming and she swallows. She shouldn't have spoken. It came out all wrong. Yossi is frowning at the road ahead. He has misunderstood her.

Claire leans on the window, exhausted from smiling and trying to be nice, when all the time she's terrified. They're passing through farmland now, folded green hills, drawing further and further away from Roimata, leaving her with these strangers. She watches for a while and then closes her eyes.

24

YOSSI

HE ALMOST RESISTS THE TEMPTATION. Sitting out in the sun on the front step Yossi puts his bowl of muesli down and taps out a text cancelling the meeting. But he can't send it. The allure of knowing more about Claire's childhood, the tantalising possibility of solving the mystery and being able to tell Claire is too much. Just one more time.

He sets off early so that he can walk. He looks up. Can't see a single cloud. The glare from the pavement, the vivid hibiscus, and the buzz of light planes overhead all add up to a delicious sense of wellbeing.

The address is a tired-looking villa in Newton Gully. A cat stretches on the verandah in the sunshine as Yossi knocks on a wooden door that needs a coat of paint. A guy with blonde surfie hair answers, but he's talking on the phone so he gestures for Yossi to follow him down the dark hallway.

They emerge into a light-filled kitchen, painted a mossy green. On the wooden table, papers and newspaper clippings surround a perfect flowering moth orchid. Next to the table there's a whiteboard, ruled into a schedule. Through the window, in Newton Gully, vast concrete motorways tangle, cars crawl past without end, divide, come together again, against a background of bare dirt and graffiti-scarred underpasses.

Simon finishes his call, apologises, introduces himself, and makes a pot of tea. Yossi stares at the whiteboard. It's a timeline for January 1970, the year of Kathryn Phillips' disappearance. January the 27th has a red star on it and a photo of a young girl riding a horse. Yossi realises that it must be Kathryn Phillips. He's only ever seen the one photo of the girl, the one he guesses her parents must have released to the media when she went missing. A smiling girl. Pretty and innocent. He guesses this photo was the reason the case lingered so long in people's memories. What would have happened had they released this one instead, he wonders, looking at a photo where Kathryn, her hands knotted in the horse's mane, looks less blonde, less pretty, more ordinary?

There's lots of scribbling on the whiteboard schedule. *PB – fight with R? PB – car to garage.* PB? Oh, that was Claire's father, Patrick Bowerman.

Simon puts a cup of tea down beside Yossi and hands him a worn folder.

On the front cover a white sticker bears the legend *Claire Rita Bowerman, b.1969*. It's mostly photocopied newspaper reports.

Aged seventeen. Claire Bowerman, daughter of pardoned murderer Patrick Bowerman, scored the top University Scholarship mark in Auckland for biology. From the sixth form. The photo, Claire turning up to the Town Hall prizegiving alone, wearing a baggy checked skirt, perhaps her mother's, and sneakers, using a hand to shield her face from the camera.

Aged twenty-two. A report of her mother's death by suicide. A picture of a young girl walking alongside a coffin carried by men in suits. She is tiny and grainy on a long lens, but the caption tells him it is Claire.

Yossi sips his tea, which tastes of bergamot. It's bracing and deliciously citrusy, but bloody hot and it burns first his tongue then the back of his throat. He can hear Simon bustling about in the kitchen.

Her mother killed herself? He can't believe he didn't know this. How could she not have told him this? She feels like a stranger, this girl who keeps so much to herself. His poor, dear Claire.

How can he pretend now that he doesn't know this secret she keeps?

25

AUCKLAND 1983

Even though there's drizzly rain, which seems to have been there for weeks, Claire dawdles home on her bike after school, coasting, only pedalling every so often. There are a few good puddles to go through, so she speeds up for those, taking her feet off the pedals and sticking her legs out, spraying water out the sides. Her mother had said she could stay home from school that day to wait for him but she hadn't wanted to; they had a science test and she'd been studying hard. Tonight she's going to work on her speech. There's a choice of topics. She likes the one about the Treaty of Waitangi best, but she knows the other kids will laugh at her if she chooses that. They'll do anything that lets them talk about their pets, or Spandau Ballet.

Her father sits at their kauri table, reading the newspaper. He drinks coffee and picks his teeth with a small piece of cardboard he's folded over. When he beckons her and hugs her to him, he's still holding the cardboard. Yuk. His face is stubbly. His hair sticks up at the front in a strong cowlick, exactly like hers. His skinny legs are pale in his loose walk shorts. They're a bit gross, his legs, sort of baggy. The collar of his blue shirt is wearing thin, fraying along the fold. She wants to touch the frayed bit to her cheek because it looks so soft.

Her mother peels carrots. Claire goes to help.

"No, it's ok, sit down and talk to your father."

Claire's stomach tightens.

She gets herself two biscuits and sits down by her father. He folds the newspaper neatly.

"Claire, I'm moving back in. Your mother's giving me another chance."

Her mother's giggly and happy. She sings *Total Eclipse Of The Heart* while she does the housework. The prowlers have stopped coming. Mum says it's because they have seen a man about the house again. Dinners get good. Steak with mushroom and wine sauce, pork chops, pot roast. Claire feels slightly lost without her cooking and cleaning jobs, but it gives her extra time to study. When she tells her father she's going to go to medical school, he says he's proud but not to expect much help from him because he is not clever.

While he'd been in prison, her mother had smashed most of Patrick's records with a rolling pin, in small bursts of rage. Every so often Claire had sneaked in, taken a pile of the spared ones and stored them in a high cupboard in her bedroom.

One night, while her mother's out trying a new prayer group, Claire asks her father to come to her room. The cupboard is really hard to get to but she can climb up there by standing on tiptoes on the built-in dressing table. Self-conscious about her thirteen-year-old body, she stretches up, leaning on her wallpaper with its stripes of blue roses. She hands the pile of twenty or so worn and well-loved records down to her father a few at a time. He makes strange gasping sounds as he looks at each one.

"I didn't know which were your favourites, so I just grabbed a pile, sorry."

When the LP of Faure's Requiem comes down, he puts the others on the bed and holds that one up and makes 'oh' noises and there are tears in his eyes. She looks at the title, memorising it, wondering how you say that word. Four-ay. Four-ray. Fooor.

He goes into his room and comes back with a cassette player and a pile of tapes of classical music and gives them all to her, showing her how to insert and eject the tapes and how to press Play. She can't believe it. Her own music in her own room. She knows that the player and tapes are from his prison cell, though they never talk about it. She's glad he had some music in there. She wonders who got it for him but she's too shy to ask.

Claire does homework in her room each night after dinner. She's doing a project on Mendel, illustrating the pages with detailed botanical drawings of the pea plants, which she copies out of their encyclopedia set. The other kids mock her in class for using the word heterozygous, but she doesn't care. She loves science and she loves her funny, clever science teacher, Mr Sutherland. She daydreams of living, like Mendel, in a monastery with a huge garden, where the monks sing and chant at night, and everything is peaceful.

Each night, her parents argue. Her father's often drunk, slurring his words and swearing. Claire learns to shut the noises out and work on her project. She listens to all her Dad's tapes, the volume down low because she doesn't want her mother to take them off her. The music makes her happy inside and blocks out the arguing a bit. At least she's free to study without the usual constant interruptions from her mother.

One night, her mother screams that Mr Gardiner around the corner is spying on them. Patrick refuses to go with her to confront him, so she goes alone, but only after huge hysterics. Karen Gardiner's in Claire's year at school. Neither of them say anything to each other the next day or even look at each other. It's embarrassing because they both play keyboards in the school orchestra and at assembly they have to play the marimba together. Claire feels herself go red in the face while she hits the wooden keys during *Jamaica Farewell*.

A few days later, when she gets home from orchestra practice, her father's gone and his records have gone with him. She sits on her bed, holding the tape player and cassettes. Her mother says nothing about why Dad has left.

Life goes back to normal. Macaroni cheese, spaghetti on toast, boiled eggs.

For the rest of her life Faure will bring to mind her father. As an adult, she hears the Requiem in London, at St Martin-in-the-Fields. The soprano sings from up in the gallery behind the congregation and the music echoes around the ancient church, around and about her, filling her senses, mournful and glorious.

26

STARSHIP HOSPITAL 2010

CLAIRE'S EXAMINING A SEVEN-YEAR-OLD, the apple of his mother's eye, in the same room as Triumph and Che. She palpates his cold abdomen using the flat of her hand, superimposing the fingers from her other hand for an even distribution of pressure, watching his face for signs of discomfort.

In her peripheral vision a woman in light blue scrubs and red Crocs, wheels her trolley over to Triumph's side and starts pulling on rubber gloves. She's here to take his blood. A photo of a cat is taped to her trolley. She has a cheerful, I'm-here-to-do-my-job manner. And a loud voice to match.

"Hi dear one, can you hold out your arm? Mum, it's best if you hold onto the arm and keep it still for me."

Claire keeps pressing, left to right, top to bottom, in her own personal routine. She feels for the liver, pressing hard when the boy displays no discomfort.

Triumph recognises the woman. She's stuck him with a needle before. He's not silly.

"No needle. Go away."

Claire glances over. Patch has her hand on Triumph's head.

"Now, the doctor wants to look at your blood and see what it can tell us to help you get better. It's just a small prick. It won't hurt for long. Then you can have a lolly. Look, this is my cat. He's called Giles."

"No. No prick. No." He slaps her hand away with a growl.

"Son. You have to do it," Patch says, her voice harsh and guttural.

"No!" In anticipation of defeat, the tears come.

Knockers leans over lazily and slaps Triumph's hand hard with his huge tattooed one. "Put out your fuckin' arm," he growls.

Triumph holds out his arm and the phlebotomist wastes no time jabbing.

When his face crumples, Knockers glares at him. "Don't fuckin' cry." He watches the boy, holds up his hand as if to strike, daring him to show weakness. "Don't cry!"

He doesn't cry.

The mother she's with looks at Claire in consternation, as though she will share a little conspiratorial, middle-class despair at the antics of these aliens. Rolling her eyes, tut-tutting. Wondering whether Claire will do something. Claire pretends she hasn't seen.

Claire tells Janet about it later.

"Some would say that's good parenting for the life he's likely to lead. He won't last long living with the Mob if he cries at every knock," Janet says.

But he's three years old.

Already late leaving, Claire finds Che MacKenzie alone again. There's really no medical reason to keep him. She looks at his charts, almost hoping she can find an excuse.

On a shelf near his bed someone's put some books. She picks one up. *A Summery Saturday Morning*. She sits down and reads it to him. He just stares at her. A nurse comes in and does a double take.

"Oh, Doctor, um – did you need anything?"

Claire ignores her.

"What's sand?" Che asks.

"Sand," Claire says, "you know, at the beach, beside the sea."

He looks at her blankly.

She has to get home. Roimata's coming back from the marae with Rachel. She can't wait to see her.

At about eight Roimata bounces in, gives Claire a nod and lopes up to her bedroom with her bag. Rachel comes in too.

"How did she go?" asks Claire.

"She's a lovely girl. A real hit with the whānau. Seems to take it all in her stride. Claire, I hope you don't mind, but Brent talked to Roi on the phone last night."

What? No. Claire starts cleaning up Yossi's cooking mess. She bites her lip hard. It's left to Yossi to see Rachel out. As they leave the kitchen Rachel comes over to Claire and takes her arm.

"Brent's a good man. He will be careful."

Claire shrugs her hand off and doesn't say goodbye.

Yossi comes back in and puts his arms around her.

"I can't believe she did that. It's outrageous," Claire says.

"Had to happen sometime –"

"But it's not her choice when."

"We don't own our children, Claire."

What? Since when did Yossi start talking like a Hallmark card? She shrugs him off and starts to set the table. Why can't he see that they need to protect Roimata?

Claire puts down her knife and fork, finishes chewing and says to Roimata, "How was it, Roi-Roi?"

"It was so cool, Mum. They told me all about my whakapapa – my genealogy – but I can't remember it all. I liked it Mum."

"Did they party a lot?"

Even as she says it, Claire hears how it sounds.

Yossi frowns at her.

"What do you mean?" Roimata says.

"Was there a lot of drinking? Sorry, I'm just an over-protective mum. You've never stayed so far away from me before."

"You don't trust me. And just because they're Māori doesn't mean they're drinking and taking drugs. God, Mum."

Roimata stares at her, her eyes wide.

"It's not that. You're only fifteen."

Claire remembers when she was a teenager. East Coast. Drug capital of New Zealand. Rastas on horses. Mysterious fires. Policemen run out of town.

"Mum, I was thinking. Now that I've met the Te Hiras, what

about your family? Isn't there anyone I can meet from your side?"

She's still staring at Claire, almost daring her to react.

Claire pretends to be concentrating on separating the delicate layers of filo pastry in Yossi's spanakopita. "No. Sorry. There's only me."

"Your Dad's still alive though. Charlotte saw him on TV."

"Yes and I told you I have nothing to do with him. I'm sorry if it sounds harsh. Really, I've been better off without him." She doesn't like the way Yossi is looking at her, either.

"You're so hard." Roi gets up and rinses her plate, without excusing herself. She thumps heavily up the stairs to her room.

Hard? Is that what she is?

When she and Yossi are loading the dishwasher he says, "What Roi said about your father –"

"No. Ok?"

"Ok," says Yossi, "but it's sad."

"I'm fine with it. I thought you got that."

She knocks on Roi's door.

"Can I come in?"

Roi is sitting on the bed, watching something on her laptop. She doesn't look up.

Above her a huge noticeboard, crammed with photos of Roimata and her friends from London, dressed up, being silly, wearing hats. There are tickets and cards and postcards and letters and drawings. Dried flowers, bits of ribbon. On her bedside table, a new framed enlargement of the photo of Brent in front of the Eiffel Tower. Another of Brent and his two daughters, posing for a studio photo. Surrounded by make-up, bottles of nail polish, books.

"Roi, you spoke to Brent."

Roi nods.

"Pause that, Roi."

Roi does press Pause. Then she smoothes out her red quilt and traces the black calligraphy with her finger. The Chinese characters mean something like Peace, Love and Friendship.

"What was that like, speaking to him? It must have been weird for you."

Claire sits down on the edge of the bed but Roi doesn't move to make room for her.

"It was ok."

"Roi. What was it like? What did you talk about?"

Roi shrugs.

"Did it feel strange?" Claire says.

"It was ok." She keeps looking down at her fingers.

"I love you Roi." She leaves the girl to her computer. "If you want to talk about it, I'm here."

Claire's writing up notes in her study later in the evening when her mobile rings. An overseas number she doesn't recognize. She presses Reject. A few moments later it beeps and there's a voice message.

Ah, Claire. Whoa! This is weird. I don't know what to say. My name's Brent Te Hira. Last time I saw you we were in Florence, a long time ago. Rachel Rakena's my sister. I'd like to talk. Ring me on this number. I'm coming to New Zealand.

27

On the day she is to meet Brent, Claire wakes up to drizzly weather. Bugger, she's arranged to see him at Western Springs Park, a twenty-minute drive from the hospital, on the other side of town, because she's unlikely to see anyone she knows. She hadn't thought about what they would do if it rained. She changes clothes several times. Pencil skirt and heels designed to make her look professional and business-like. Too fake. A dress she likes. Too try-hard. She settles on her usual jeans and a pretty blue cardigan that she's been told suits her. She wants to feel comfortable.

The day holds dread for her in a few ways, but it's meeting Brent again she can't stop thinking about as she drives to work.

Che MacKenzie's back. The child she'd flagged in a meeting a few weeks ago, the one she thought was being abused. They all thought was being abused. The decision had been made to 'monitor' the family. Whatever that means.

Claire's been called to the ED to examine Che's abdomen. His mother is there, all bleached hair and thick make-up. One of those top-heavy women, Heaven has squeezed her enormous bust and arms into a tight black shirt; aware her leopard print mini-skirt reveals shapely legs. There's a man with Heaven and she glances at him all the time, flirtatious and needy. The thin man reeks of body odour and stale cigarette smoke. He's shaved his head and has an arrogant stance and a belligerent manner to match. Rolling from foot to foot, he can't seem to stand still. He snaps at Claire when she speaks to Heaven without looking at him.

"Show me some respect."

She knows these men. Saw them in England. Great self-esteem but meagre self-respect. They believe in standing up for things, for their own rights, but it seems to be the right to act on a whim, not any rights worth fighting for. He's making a lot of noise, self-righteous complaining.

She glances at the notes. Query retinal haemorrhage. Che's been bashed again then. Asking the man to excuse her, Claire pushes past him to look at Che, who's lying with his eyes closed but conscious. Are those cigarette burns up the arms? Could they just be infected fleabites? There are marks on his legs, bruising, consistent with a belt.

Claire's job is to check for internal injuries. She palpates his belly. He's probably ok. Look at his ears, though. Subtle bruising of the pinna. Almost nothing bruises the ear like this except abuse. Being held and wrung and pulled. There's a thick ring of dirt behind his ears from days of not washing. This dirt almost undoes Claire. These things are not the preserve of a surgeon, but she could have prevented this. She knew this last week when she saw this child.

"Has the ophthalmologist seen him?" she says to the nurse.

"Not yet."

"I want him admitted to the surgical ward. And I want Te Puaruruhau involved." That's the Child Abuse team but she's hoping the caregivers don't know that.

"Diagnosis?"

The nurse wants a diagnosis for the form. Claire has to think quickly. Che doesn't need surgery this time but, boy, he needs to be kept in the hospital. In case the eye people don't admit him, she will.

"Trauma to abdomen."

She leaves the room and goes straight to the social work office to make sure this has been reported, where, just her luck, she finds the social worker who had argued with her over the Peteru case.

"We'll take care of it," is her answer.

"Have the police been notified?"

"Not yet. We are arranging a meeting with the family. We'll draw up a plan at the case conference tomorrow. It's not certain yet."

"There are injuries to his eye and to his ears that are rarely accidental. He must not go home with these people. We've discussed him before. How many admissions does he need? Are we going to wait until they kill him?"

"We're all upset. Leave it to us please. We'll leave the medical stuff to you. And try not to be so judgmental. I could tell you a few things about Heaven, ok? She's had a tough life."

Claire knows Che's mother's unlikely to be a demon. She assumes her childhood was tough. It shows in her face. It's etched into her stance and the attitude of her head. Jesus. That doesn't help Che.

It's stopped raining but she's late for Brent. He's waiting at the picnic table closest to the zoo, as they'd arranged. A complete stranger. She's been wondering if there'll be an intimacy, a connection with this man she's thought about so much but no, he's a stranger.

Hurrying to get there has left her flustered and hot and sticky. She apologises too many times for being late and he motions for her to sit down next to him.

"I'll get you a coffee," he says, and walks over and orders at the kiosk nearby without asking her what she would like. Then he comes back over, smiling at her. "The coffee might be a few minutes," he says.

He's put on weight. His hair's too long. Still the perfect skin and features though. White teeth in a smile that she knows can make you feel you're the only person in the room. Black leather jacket, crisp white shirt, neat jeans, polished black leather biker boots.

There are children and young mothers everywhere, mostly in groups with huge pushchairs and bags full of jackets and food and toys. The ducks are screeching. The smell of duck poo mingles with the smell of hot chips from the kiosk. Toddlers yell and laugh. She feels out of place, furtive, as though she's doing something wrong.

She tries to stop herself staring at Brent, looking for elements of Roimata, of course. Something about the way the head is held, the curve of the cheek hollow, the slightly amused default expression of the mouth. And a lot more too.

All those ridiculous false dichotomies. Nature versus Nurture. Genes versus Experience. As if it could possibly be one or the other. She knows it's a complex interaction, a random, inelegant dance.

Brent has that outgoing, intelligent engagement with her that she and Yossi find so interesting in Roimata. She and Yossi have nurtured it, turning it into wisdom, taste and caring. What a pointless exercise, this trying to unravel is. She can't help indulging in it anyway.

When Brent goes to collect their coffees he spills the contents of his wallet onto the ground, coins rolling in the trampled mud, credit cards falling everywhere. Unperturbed, he holds his head back and laughs out loud, rolling his eyes at his own clumsiness. Exactly how Roimata would react. When he bends down to pick it all up he says something to a toddler waiting in the queue that makes the child giggle and the mother leans down and helps Brent pick up his money, handing it to him with a smitten smile, showing lots of her long slender neck to Brent. That easy charm, that comfort in his own skin, was what Claire had responded to in Italy. Confidence like that is so seductive. And she's seen it work for Roimata too, though not yet with the strong sexual element that Brent has.

For Roimata it is this signal she sends, that the world is joyful, that she soaks up experience. People everywhere want to be with her, want some of her light to fall on them. Her own goodwill, worn on the outside without a shred of distrust or cynicism, brings out goodwill and joy in others. Claire has wondered whether it's as simple as being good-looking. But she's sure it's not. Though that no doubt helps.

Brent sits down again.

"You look just the same, but I guess you're more real. Memories are weird things, aren't they?" he says.

He's the first to bring up Roimata.

"I talked to your daughter."

Your daughter. That's gracious of him.

"I'm sorry I've never told you. I just didn't know what to do. You were married, you had other children," Claire says.

"It's been a shock but it's a nice shock. Rach would've told you that my wife, Marita, died about seven years ago."

Claire nods. Sips her cappuccino.

"It's true it would have broken her heart," he continues. "But I think I'll tell my daughters about Roimata. I think they'll forgive me. A different generation. A new half-sister."

Claire winces. More people to complicate Roimata's life.

"Are you here for long?" she asks.

"Three months. I took a whole lot of leave from work."

Oh dear. They are really going to have to face this.

"Not just because of Roimata. I was going to do it soon anyway. Come home for a while."

A wee boy, riding his trike around the track with his legs pumping, falls off and screams. His tired looking mother puts the baby she's holding back in the pram and races over to pick him up. He's snotty and bleeding and covered in pieces of the bark that forms the soft landing pad for the playground. But the mother hugs him close to her clean white blouse, not caring. Straight away his screams die down to snotty sobs. Claire misses those moments.

"I'm amazed you called her Roimata."

"I remembered you talking about your grandmother that day."

"Tell me about Roimata," he says.

"Hasn't Rachel told you what she's like?"

"I can't believe – all these years – I'm trying to imagine –"

"It's all been pretty normal. She plays the violin. She's a good chess player. She's healthy."

"You have a partner?"

"Yes, Yossi. He's been with us since before she went to school. He's like a father to her. We're a family. I'm sorry."

He holds up both hands. "That's cool. I'm glad she's had a father. I'd like to meet her though? I didn't tell her I was coming over, just got on a plane."

Claire walks over to the bin and dumps her empty cup. She

goes back, picks up her bag. She needs to check on the girl she's just operated on.

"Look, I need to think about this, ok? I need to talk to Yossi. Roimata's already had to adjust to moving here, leaving all her friends. It's not a good time for us right now. There's a lot going on."

"I promise, I won't try and be a Dad or anything. I just want to meet her, to see her. To be, well, like a friend really."

He's being so nice.

"I'll think about it," Claire says.

He stands up, grabs both her hands and looks into her eyes. He's very good-looking still.

"Claire. Thanks for meeting with me. And with Rachel. I know you didn't have to. It's been great to see you again. I have happy memories of Florence."

Flustered again, she studies her watch and then walks so fast to her car that she's almost running.

Claire slips in beside Yossi that night. He's fast asleep and she warms her frozen feet on his calves. When she wakes, he's handing her a cup of tea.

She tells him about Che MacKenzie, how someone has beaten him.

"Claire, I know you. I know you do what you can. You'll treat him with tenderness and love now. That will help him become strong."

Yossi often talks like this, about hearts and trust and tenderness. His language is demonstrative. It doesn't mean she ever gets any closer to him or understands him any more than other men in her life. But sometimes she can even believe he'll stay with her, stay loving like this.

"I can't believe those parents hurt that child. I was so lucky. My parents were lovely," he says, "so caring. I would never ever have left if my parents had been alive. But I had given up on Israel. Given up on there ever being a resolution. Only forgetting can do it."

"I feel guilty about your parents," Claire says.

"Why?"

"Oh you know, only thousands of years of battling for Jewish identity. All those generations and we break it. Don't you feel the weight of all that?" she asks.

"How do I help they who no longer exist by being miserable myself?"

He's right, of course. But she still feels guilty. His parents sound so amazing. She wishes she could have met them.

28

YOSSI

"Yossi, it's Rachel. Have you got a moment?"

"Yes."

"It's about Roi."

"Hold on a minute."

Yossi puts the phone down, turns off the pan where he is browning lamb, puts a lid on it. He picks up the phone again and sits at the kitchen table.

"Is she all right?"

"It's this business with Claire's father, Patrick Bowerman. Roimata has talked to him and she's going to meet him."

Oh God, Claire is going to hit the roof.

"I said she must tell you, or I would," Rachel continues. "I hope that was the right thing to say. I'm so sorry. She's very stubborn."

He walks to the open kitchen door and stands just outside in the sun and closes his eyes.

"I want her to trust me, Yossi. But I thought you should know."

"Thanks so much."

After school Yossi makes Roimata chai and cookies. She announces the plan as a *fait accompli*.

"Yoss, guess what? I've found Mum's father. His name's Patrick Bowerman. I phoned him. I've arranged to see him after school on Monday. In a café."

"Roimata. I am glad you are being open with me. But your Mum doesn't want this."

"He can't help what happened to him. He was pardoned. It's my decision."

"You're meeting your – Brent Te Hira – tomorrow, Roi. It'll be emotional for all of us. Can we just deal with one thing at a time?"

"She can't stop me. I really want to see what he's like. She's so judgmental."

"That's not fair, Roimata. She's been hurt. You don't know all that's happened to her. She's really strong, actually."

"It's not all about Mum. She can't stop me. I'm going. I hate her. I hate her." Roimata stalks out of the room.

He follows her.

"Roimata, I'll come with you."

She's stopped on the stairs, but with her back to him.

"I'm not a baby."

"Roi, he was a convicted criminal."

She turns around.

"He was pardoned. Simon Flaxstone says he's innocent. Yossi don't tell Mum or I'll never forgive you. She'll stop me going."

"Ok. I won't tell Claire, provided you promise to let me come with you." Roimata sighs a dramatic sigh as she continues upstairs.

What has he done? This is getting out of control.

29

YOSSI

"Did you read about the protests at the Wigmore Hall?" Arie leans forward on his spade, wiping his forehead with his garden glove.

Yossi is helping Arie lay an irrigation system in his Meadowbank garden. They're dressed the same. Baggy shorts to their knees, shirtless, sunglasses against the brightness, and heavy work boots. Yossi already has a dull ache in his shoulder from digging. Every so often, when they try out their trenches by running the hose, they get sprayed with freezing water and Yossi is grateful for the cooling down.

"They just want attention. I read their blog," Arie continues.

"Me too. So sad." Yossi stops digging and crouches down to rescue a delicate white cosmos plant, which is being strangled by clover but is flowering anyway. He disentangles it gently, staring at it for a moment before laying it down nearby to be replanted. He'd read with horror about the protests last night.

"Those guys play with Arab musicians in the East-West Orchestra. They're not even all Israeli," says Arie.

"I know." Yossi smashes his spade into the gravelly soil.

Yesterday at the Wigmore Hall, a haven of old-fashioned decorum in spite of being just off Oxford Street, four or five members of the audience had shouted slogans to interrupt a concert by the Jerusalem Quartet. Security guards had hustled each protestor out and the concert had resumed, only to be interrupted by another protest from a different part of the Hall. Yossi can imagine the scene, the perfect acoustics, the beautiful music, the ugly interruptions. Many of the audience were probably older people. They would have been angry, bewildered. It makes him sick to his stomach.

"Let's just lay out some more of this stuff," Arie says, feeding out the black poly-tubing. It twists and snakes as he tries to plan where it will feed water. "Not sure about some of these joins."

"I know," says Yossi, crouching down and trying to attach a nozzle. "If we can get it over there, you'll be able to have another flowerbed."

"Has Roimata met that guy Brent yet?"

"It's today."

"Really? How do you feel about it?"

How does he feel about it? It just needs to be done.

"He's her father."

"I disagree. You're her father. He should leave you all alone."

Yossi just shrugs. He presses hard, forcing a plastic connection to the hose with a clear click.

"You seemed upset the other day?" asks Arie.

"Yeah. Claire met him without telling me first. But I'm over that now." Yossi remembers his jealousy and hurt. She's still hiding things from him. It was never like this in London.

"Aren't you worried about Roimata having divided loyalties?"

"I'm cool with it. I don't know why. Just am."

Yossi picks up the hose, his back to Arie.

"How's it going with that girl you met?" he teases.

"Rebecca. She's great," Arie laughs. "She's moving in here."

"Oh, so that's why you want a garden! To impress her! She's Jewish?"

"Yep. Makes it easy. I want to have babies with her."

Yossi spins around and aims the hose at Arie, drenching him and laughing.

"You vill have many beautiful Jewish babies," he says, broadening his accent and sounding like an old Yiddish matchmaker.

Later, Arie hands Yossi a beer and they sit down on a low stone wall in the shade, both streaky with dirt and sweat, their hands and shorts filthy. Yossi look at the results of their morning's work, neatly filled in trenches, topsoil replaced, the new system sprinkling cool water with a soothing hiss.

"I can't stop thinking about that concert. It's sacrilege. Music, of all things," Arie says. "It brings people together. And during Pesach too. Maybe you should write a blog about it?"

Yossi shrugs, aware of a sharp pain in his shoulder blade. He'd told Claire about the Wigmore thing last night. She'd been distracted, hardly listened. Why didn't she understand his hurt?

"It was a peaceful protest," she'd said. "No-one was hurt. You can't blame them really. Israel is being outrageous."

She'd turned away.

30

Surely Roi will be anxious about meeting Brent. Claire waits for her to talk about it, but at about eleven-thirty Roi comes out of her room, carrying her best red Marcs bag, slightly more make-up than usual the only sign she's feeling any different from any other day. She's dressed casually, as she usually is. Jeans and a t-shirt with a big globe and the slogan, *There is no Planet B*. Comfortable in her own skin. If she's worried about it at all, she's hiding it well.

Claire checks again whether she'd like company. Maybe there are last minute nerves.

"My heart's beating fast," Roi says, "but I'd still rather go on my own."

Independent genes. Where could she have got those? Claire laughs to herself, desperate to normalise this.

"Bye Mum."

"I can give you a lift if you like?"

"Nah. It's ok. I'll get the bus."

"How are you going to know him? Is he wearing a red carnation?" Trying to sound light-hearted but just sounding naff.

"I've seen heaps of photos."

"Darling. You'll know him straight away. You look so like him. Don't get a fright. This is going to be strange for you."

"I love you Mum."

Then she's gone.

When Debs had suggested they go out for coffee while Roi was meeting Brent, she'd said no. Now she wishes she'd said yes. She feels like shite. She'd been a bit shocked when Yossi had gone off to help Arie in his garden. She had thought he'd be home with her.

She's sorely tempted to follow Roi, and watch from afar. Make sure they don't see her. But she won't. She mustn't.

She fills the sink with steaming water and a splash of bleach. Scrubs the sink and the taps and the benches. That wonderful clean smell. Probably killing off brain cells. She takes a cup of tea out into the hot garden and wills herself to sit still and drink it. She can't control this. Roimata has her own life, must be allowed to form her own relationship with this man, so intimately connected to her, yet a stranger.

The phone rings.

"Kia ora." It's Rachel Rakena.

"Hello."

"It's a big day for you."

"I'm fine thank you."

"Can I come and pick you up, take you for a coffee?"

"No no, I'm all right."

"Go on. I'd love to see you. I'll pick you up in about fifteen."

She's gone.

She's met her match in this Rachel. But it will, at least, be a distraction.

Rachel arrives with a bunch of flowers from her garden. They go to a local garden centre, drink several flat whites each and eat berry friands. Rachel reassures her that her brother's a good man. She's so nice. So calm and reasonable. Claire realises she is becoming very fond of Rachel, in spite of herself. Rachel seems to get her.

"I know I upset you when I let her talk to Brent. But it was going to happen, Claire. You can't control everything."

It's lovely sitting in the shade and looking at all the potted flowers. Water trickles into a pond nearby. Roimata is meeting Brent. This is something Claire has thought would never happen. She will just have to trust him. Or at least trust Rachel that Brent is a good man. It's not so bad, actually. If Yossi can cope with this, she can too.

When Roi gets home she doesn't say much.

"How was it?" Claire tries to sound casual.

"It was fine. He's really nice. He's so like Aunty Rachel." Roimata goes upstairs, gets out her violin and starts to practise. Good move. She knows Claire never interrupts that.

But no, violin can wait today. Claire goes up and hesitates outside Roi's bedroom door before knocking and going in. "Roi –"

"Mmm?" Roi rosins her bow with long thin fingers that she certainly didn't get from Claire.

"You're playing the quaver run and the semi-quaver run at the same speed. Slow the quavers down. Pa pom pom pom pom pom," says Claire.

"Oh yeah."

"Roi – you know if you want to talk –"

"I'm fine. Hey, guess what? He loves chess. That's so weird. I thought I got that from Yossi."

"It was the first thing Yossi noticed about you. The way you stared at his chess game in the shop. Weird indeed. But Yossi taught you to play."

"Yeah and Yossi's a lot better player than Brent sounds. He said he's a bunny."

As Claire turns to go, Roi says, "I love you, Mum."

What a fantastic kid she's got. They'll get through this. Just Yossi, Roi and her against the world. The way it used to be.

31

YOSSI

Yossi and Roimata stand in the doorway of the grim café in Great North Road, peering inside. Four or five loud young men in hoodies and sneakers swear and laugh, leaning on the tables on the pavement, almost blocking their way. Yossi glares at them. When Roi said she'd agreed to meet Patrick, Yossi had never heard of the café. He'd assumed, when he'd heard Grey Lynn, that it was an Allpress and brioche affair. Instead it's part of some middle of the road chain. This particular one, surrounded as it is by smarter outfits, has found a niche with the poor, the mad and the homeless. The coffee is cheap.

"There he is," says Roi, pointing.

"How do you know that's him?" asks Yossi, hoping she's got it wrong.

"He told me he'd be sitting at his favourite table, underneath a poster of Marilyn Monroe."

Sure enough, on the wall above the old man, a garish poster. It's one of the vulnerable ones, her clothes too tight, her hair too blonde, her face too perfect.

Roi strides over to the corner where the man, his thin hair long down the back of his ancient t-shirt, fidgets with a coffee cup.

Yossi waits and watches Roi speak to the old man, who jumps up and embraces her. Now Yossi wants to get to her but he has to push past an elderly couple and their shopping spread all around them on the floor.

"This is Yossi, my dad," Roimata says.

The old man puts out his hand for Yossi to shake. "Hello, delighted to meet you. Isn't it a stunning day?"

Yossi wants coffee even though he knows it will be terrible. "I'll order some drinks. Roi, would you like a hot chocolate? Would you like anything, sir?"

"Yes, actually. There was some rather delicious looking ginger crunch. Would you be kind enough to get me some?"

When Yossi returns after paying the sullen girl at the counter, Patrick is telling Roi about his schooldays. His reddened eyes flick about a lot. Scabs litter his dirty face and he gives off a sour wet carpet smell. It's been weeks since the lank hair has seen shampoo. But is this a man capable of evil?

Then Patrick is talking to Yossi. "Please tell me about my daughter. How is she?"

Yossi places a hand on the emaciated arm. The skin feels tissue thin.

"Your daughter's a beautiful woman you can be proud of, sir. She's a doctor. She's a great mother and a kind and generous person."

And I love her and I am going to marry her, he wants to add. He must keep that to himself, though, because Patrick will not be invited. Which is making Yossi feel uncomfortable. Weddings bring out forgiveness in people. Yossi has seen it. Weddings and births can bring hope and redemption.

The waiter arrives with their coffees. The old man takes his ginger crunch, picks up the whole over-sized piece and takes a bite. Then, talking through the food, says to Roi, "You said on the phone that you play chess. You might have got that from me. I was very good at games."

Roi leans forward and starts to tell him a few of her triumphs. She's normally modest, but she tells her grandfather about the cup she won, that she was the best player in the chess club at school in London.

He interrupts her. "I have to go now. Sorry." He stands.

Roi and Yossi cross the road with him. With each breath out, he makes a wheezy grunt. At the car he says, "So lovely to meet you both." He touches Roi on the arm. "You are very beautiful, my dear." Then he turns to Yossi. "Look, this is rather embarrassing but I seem to have forgotten my wallet. Would you be good enough to lend me some money for lunch?"

What? Yossi reaches into his wallet and realises he has only small change and a one hundred dollar note. He hands the note to Patrick, who shrugs and walks away, hunched over against the wind, down Great North Road towards the city. Yossi turns to Roi and smiles, opens the car door for her.

There's yelling and shouting. Loud, malignant shouting. It's coming from around the corner, where Patrick has just disappeared from view.

Yossi runs. Roi runs just behind him.

Patrick sprawls face down on the rough, gravelly footpath, a skinny boy kicking him in the head, swinging his foot back furiously in between each kick.

"Mothafucka. We saw you on TV."

Another boy watches, smiling, the hundred dollar note in his hand.

Roi grabs the head-kicker.

"Stop it! Stop! What are you doing?"

He pushes her away with one hand.

"What's happening here? Stop this at once." Yossi tries to take control now.

The head-kicker puts another kick in.

"Fuck off, cunt. It's fuckin' nuthin'. He killed a fuckin' girl, eh?"

Each ugly 'fuckin' is accompanied by a savage, sickening boot to Patrick's stomach.

Yossi shoulder charges the kicker's chest and grabs the pumping leg.

"Don't. Stop this right now. He's an old man."

The smiling boy pulls the hood of his sweatshirt over his head and holds up his hand in a stop gesture. "Bro, it's cool bro. He killed that hitchhiker. We saw him on the TV. He's always around here."

"Stop it. Stop it." This time Yossi gets between the head-kicker and Patrick but the smiler grabs his shirt and shoves him out of the way.

"Help. Help. Stop it!" Roi kneels down by Patrick, covering him with her body, her screams turning to sobs.

"Shut up, bitch, or you'll be next."

"Roimata, run to the car. Go!" Yossi says. He's trapped behind the head-kicker. He dives, pushing the boy away hard and shields Roimata with his body. The boy lurches forward and kicks out as Yossi's arm comes up to protect his face.

Cars are slowing down now and people are running towards them yelling. The boys saunter down a side street, all gangsta-roll and bravado, proud of their morning's work. Roi leans over Patrick, sobbing.

Pain begins seeping through Yossi's left arm. "Shh," he murmurs. He eases Roi back and kneels down by the old man who has been silent for some time.

Blood cakes his hair and courses down his dirty face onto the hot pavement. His eyes are closed, his nose pulverised and twisted sideways. Chips of gravel are embedded in his face like bloody stubble.

"Patrick!" Yossi shouts, but there's no response. People crowd around them.

"I've called an ambulance, mate," someone says.

The world feels surreal to Yossi. The pain, never that bad, has gone, but the spaced-out feeling is disconcerting. The pillow is too high. Claire catches his arm, which is slipping off his chest. He hasn't even noticed. She shows him how to hold onto it firmly with his other hand. The doctor is talking to him about something to do with the arm and physio or long-term care or something. He can't listen, can't focus.

"How's Patr – the old man?" he asks the policeman in the room.

The policeman looks confused.

"The man, the one who was being beaten?"

"He's been admitted to intensive care. They said he would be dead if you hadn't intervened. Your husband's a hero, Miss."

"What happened?" Claire asks.

Yossi's gut turns to liquid. He's cold. Why don't they give him another blanket? He can smell something. It's the hospital dinner trolley going past. Revolting. Food, how disgusting. And then a wave of fear. He vividly remembers the kick coming towards him, remembers blocking it, winces as he recalls the feeling, the resistance, and the sick-making crack.

"Roimata," he says.

"I'm here, Yoss."

She leans in and kisses his cheek. His senses feel overloaded. He might have to vomit. Drifting up through his mind, though, something he has to get out in the open.

"Claire, there's something we have to tell you. We didn't mean to hurt you."

32

Claire walks out through the waiting room, out through the double sliding doors into the bright glare, holding her breath. She hopes she won't see anyone she knows. She can't hear properly for a minute, but she keeps placing one foot in front of the other, aware of each step until she reaches her car, parked in glaring sunlight in the doctors' carpark. She fumbles with the lock and opens the driver's door. A wave of thick, leathery heat hits her. She climbs in, wincing as the seat scorches her bare legs. She leans forward and rests her cheek on the hot steering wheel.

33

It's getting late when she steers the boat carefully up alongside the jetty. It is Thursday. No-one's around but there's a blue and white launch she doesn't recognize moored close to the jetty, its rowboat pulled up on the pebbly beach.

It feels strange opening up the bach by herself. The floors gleam and the fridge and bathrooms are clinically clean. She loves the way things sit, waiting for humans, ready to go. Binoculars, waiting for hands. Candles, waiting for dark. The cushions laze on the window seat, their bright Pacific tivaevae so cheerful and vibrant.

She switches on the radio in time for the news. There's been another forestry accident up north. It's unfolding while she listens. Two dead and a third hurt badly. A bomb discovered in Times Square but not detonated. Airfares to Australia are going to get cheaper. Two boys have been arrested for the beating of an old man in Herne Bay yesterday. The media don't yet know it is the infamous Patrick Bowerman. There'll be a court case. Yossi and Roimata will have to be witnesses. God, she knew they shouldn't come back.

She makes herself a toasted sandwich, from bread she finds in the freezer and cheese left from last weekend. Opens a bottle of merlot and pours a glass. A breeze has come up. Pink geraniums are fluttering in the planters out on the deck, lit by the security lights. They don't make good cut flowers but she wants the flashy pink inside anyway. She gets the secateurs and opens the door. It's the first time she's felt even a slight chill in the air since she's been back in New Zealand. The geraniums smell bloody and metallic, but she takes a deep sniff.

She's glad to get inside again, the room warm from all the sun it's trapped that day. She puts the flowers in an old cracked milk jug and places them on her table. Picks up her phone. Six missed calls. Six texts. All from Yossi or Roi.

She's forgiven Roimata already. Tried to see it from her point of view. Wanting to know her granddad. Not knowing how shitty people can be and still be related to you.

But Yossi. Going behind her back like that. Does he care at all about what she wants? She feels guilty leaving him with his sore arm.

She looks out winter duvets and puts them by the door, so she'll remember to air them the next day. Will it be cold for the wedding? Shit, the wedding. Can she marry someone she can't trust? Can she marry anyone at all? Doesn't it give them so much power to hurt you? Wrapping a fleecy blanket around her shoulders, she heads out to the deck with her merlot, thinking she may as well watch the sun set. The sea brightens for a moment, so quickly she wonders if she imagined it, then it's cold. There's a thin stripe of yellow in the sky above the Waitakeres.

The Sky Tower appears and disappears, a vertical strip of blinking red. The lights of Auckland, hardly there a minute ago, now dominate. The water hisses softly, as though someone's left a hose on.

When she goes to bed, she swaps her jeans for pyjama pants, leaving on her bra, singlet and sweatshirt. She doesn't want to be naked even for a minute. It amazes her, when she spends time on her own, how short a time it takes to be uncivilised in the small routines, to wear her clothes to bed, to eat straight from a pot. She sleeps fitfully, waking in the night and remembering with a lurch in her stomach, that Roimata and Yossi have brought Patrick back into their lives.

Woken again by a scraping sound from behind her house, she opens the back door and she's not sure who jumps the highest, she or the elderly man in her garden, busy demolishing the rotten trellis that forms the courtyard. He looks familiar.

"Whoa!" says the man. "You gave me a fright. I didn't know anyone was here."

"Hi!"

"Sorry, I'm Joe Johnstone. I'm Debbie's dad. And you're Claire."

"Yes."

"My wife and I are staying at the bach for a while. Debs asked me to replace this rotten stuff as a surprise for you. She's bringing some new trellis over from the mainland in the weekend. I thought you were in town. I hope you don't mind."

"Oh no. Thanks so much."

"No problem. I hear you've got a wedding planned? Is there anything else you want spruced up for the big day? I like to keep busy."

"That's so nice of you."

He works away hard, although he must be nearly eighty. Claire phones in sick at work and asks another surgeon to check on a couple of her patients. She has no surgery scheduled today anyway. Feeling guilty about Joe working so hard, she starts to drag the old trellis over to her woodpile and break it up into kindling. Wants to tell him there may not even be a wedding.

"Will this be ok in my log burner?" she asks.

"Should be fine."

The work's good. It's great. She goes hard, stomping and jumping on bits to break the trellis up. It's so quiet here. The sounds they make, the satisfying thuds and splinters and cracks, ring out around the bay. Seagulls shriek.

She makes a cup of tea mid-morning and they sit outside on the deck to drink it.

"I remember you as a child," he tells her. "I remember your whole family."

She changes the subject, asking his advice on an issue they have with the water tank. He goes off to look at it.

Yossi rings all day and all evening. She presses Reject. She'd asked one thing. Don't make her think about her family. Don't drag them down into all this stuff again. She knew she shouldn't have trusted him. They should have stayed in London. She wants to go back.

34

THE BIRDS ARE WARMING UP the next morning and the dawn is poking tentative fingers into the bay when she hears Joe walk onto her deck, cough and put his bag down with a thump. Claire opens the door. She's wearing an old swanndri she found by torchlight in the laundry last night. It comes to her knees. This morning she has cut the sleeves off with scissors to a rough edge just below her elbows. Underneath, some shorts she's been using for gardening.

"Ha. Look at me. I'll drive you wild with desire in this," she says.

He grins, adjusting the belt on his baggy shorts.

The sea gleams silver and ghostly and the bush is dark on their way down the track.

"Will Joan be alright?" Debs' mother has osteoarthritis.

"Yes, she's fine. She's got a cellphone and everything she needs. I've told Debs to ring a few times and check on her."

Joe doesn't say much. Rows them out to his boat. He's a bit slow and breathless but she feels safe. He says he knows a good spot near the rocks, a few bays further south. The light stretches and yawns. He stops in an empty bay, no baches, and no boats. Just bush and rocks, all birdsong and sea-swish.

"Great during the week here, no-one much around," he says.

Claire hasn't fished for thirty years or more but she's determined to bait her own hook and kill her own fish, if she catches any. She remembers what a pain her mother used to be, always interrupting her father's fishing, demanding, talking. She wants to fish like a boy. Joe lays some squid from a packet on a cutting board criss-crossed with scrapes and hands her a sharp, clean knife. The viscous squid is cold between her fingers as she slices through it.

"That about the right size?" she asks.

"Perfect."

When the squid's in nice neat bits she wipes the knife with a rag. Joe hands her a rod he's been fiddling with. Weights, hooks, line, everything ready to go. She deftly plunges the hook into the bit of squid, twisting it and hooking it again. The squid smells salty and tangy, not yet fishy.

The water slaps against the boat but only gently. She looks hard at the reel, goes through how it works in her mind first and then flicks off the lock and sends the line out, the reel whizzing with a delicious click. When it's out far enough she snaps it locked and sits on the cushioned bench along the side of the boat. Joe's line is in too and he smiles at her. She sees how thin and dry his hair is, how his belt is slung low to be comfortable, how his bum has disappeared and there are just baggy shorts where it used to be, how one shoulder droops and the other strains to hold him up. She can remember him now as a younger man, always working, painting, gardening, and fishing. Even though they were on holiday.

While they've been getting ready, the sun has lit the bay.

"Look." Claire points out a couple of jellyfish floating past.

"Last summer there were orca out here one day. They're huge."

"I remember dolphins when I was a kid."

"Yeah, we did get them. Even came right into Ruby Bay a few times."

"Amazing."

"Yep, beautiful. You didn't get *them* in London, now, did you?"

There's a tug. It's probably just the tide, but then another and the top of her rod is bending over. She stands and winds her reel in, hears her father's voice in her head. "Give it stick. Give it stick." She turns the handle until she sees the pink glint of a snapper but when it comes to the surface it's small.

"Nah, not a keeper," says Joe.

She winds the under-size fish up above the water and leans over. Holding her rod with one hand she uses the rag to draw the wriggling fish up onto the deck, carefully anchors her rod between her knees and starts to free it as gently as she can. The fish bucks and slaps and she has to grip it hard while she works the hook out and then drops the fish back into the water.

They fish for half an hour in companionable silence before Claire feels another bite. This time it's a bigger snapper, blushing silver in the water. She stabs it in the brain, through the depression above its eye.

Joe catches two, then pours coffee from a thermos. She baits both their lines and casts them.

There's heat in the sun now and Claire leans back with her eyes closed and sips the horrible gritty instant coffee.

"Yuk," she says, "sugar."

"Sorry," he says, "I bring it pre-milked, pre-sugared. Force of habit."

"Do you actually like this disgusting instant stuff?"

"Can't see what all the fuss is about this espresso or latte or whatever. Instant is good for what ails you."

He tries to ring his wife but there's no cell phone coverage.

"We can go home if you're worried," says Claire. "I've caught my first fish in thirty years and I'm perfectly happy."

"No, no, she'll be fine. There are a few more in there yet."

"It must be hard, her getting sick," Claire says.

"Oh well, that's life," he says.

"Hard for Debs too."

"Mmm. They're close. Joan's upset about Debs being on her own now. Worries about her as we get sick and old."

"Debs is great. She'll be fine," Claire says.

"She's a good girl. Feet on the ground like her Mum. He was a loser anyway."

A couple of seagulls have found them now. Squawking and diving.

"Your Yossi, Debs says he's a good bloke."

"He is."

"Well, if he's a keeper, hold on to him tight. No fun in this world getting old alone."

With that, he rinses out their cups and packs them away. He turns his back to her and grabs his rod again, bracing his veined legs against the boat to keep his balance.

"You're a great girl, Claire. You always were. It wasn't bloody easy. I always used to say to Joan, 'She's a tough one, that one. Smart as a whippet.' Mind you, you always studied hard. You were a determined little bugger."

Claire laughs. "I still am."

"Since you've been back Joan and I have talked about what we could have done for you when you were little. Your mother – well – she was strange."

"Strange?"

"She thought people were out to get her. We didn't really know much about mental illness in those days, Claire. We used to say she was 'a bit wonky in the head'." He points to his head, his finger circling in a sign that means crazy. "But we didn't know how to help."

"My Dad –" Claire says.

"He was lost, I think. Didn't know what to do. He became very angry, stressed we'd call it now. Then they had you and that made him happy. Then–"

They both knew what happened then.

"I don't really talk about it."

"No, well, not everybody's a talker. Maybe fishing does as much good, eh?"

With that, he turns his attention back to his rod. They catch seven more fish between them, one a kahawai he'll keep for bait, the others all snapper. He's elated.

It's getting hot when he announces they've caught enough and they clean up together without talking, every so often one of them whooping or chuckling at their success.

She leans back, her head against the cabin, enjoying the rough breeze pushing against her as they motor, her body aching but warm and content. When they reach Ruby Bay she jumps into the rowboat first and grabs the oars and he lets her row them to the jetty.

"That was fantastic, thank you," she says when they reach her bach. She hugs him and kisses his cheek.

"Let me know if I can help with anything," she says.

He holds her arm as she starts to run inside. "Whatever he's done, love, forgive him," he says. "We're a long time dead." And he heads on up the track.

Whether it's the fishing, Joe's advice, or just a bit of time, Claire feels much better. She texts Yossi to say she'll come home this afternoon.

Perhaps she and Yossi should have a civilized separation. Before things get too bad and they hate each other. She always felt it wouldn't last. It's incredibly important for Roimata that they communicate and don't let their bitterness get in the way of parenting.

Her phone rings immediately.

When Yossi comes to bed that night, she's reading. She reaches for him. He holds her close and they make love. They've often done this at moments of difficulty. Neither of them is big on talking about their feelings and sex brings them close. People say you need to talk as well, and that the intimacy could be an illusion. But Claire's not sure talking is any better.

Perfectly possible to have whole conversations and not understand each other any better. Women all report talking endlessly with their partners, dragging words out of them kicking and screaming. They seem to think there are breakthroughs, when they "get" what their husbands are trying to say every so often. Claire's not so sure. She's watched the parents at work. Most men just seem to try saying different things until they find something their wife is happy with.

Tonight, she's just thrilled to be stroking and sucking and kneading this skin, this man she's not going to marry. She loves the 'presentness' of it; the way time recedes, the focus on this skin, that finger, this sensation. She loves Yossi's physical presence. He's real, flesh and blood, muscle and vein. It's confusing. But nobody is trustworthy.

When she goes back to London without him, will Roi want to come too?

35

YOSSI

Yossi is composing a song. He's got composing software on his laptop but he's hardly touched it since he came to New Zealand. He's trying not to get excited, having realised long ago that, though he has talent as a musician, he's not great.

Since visiting Patrick lying in his hospital bed, for some reason the first lines of an Allen Ginsberg poem have been going around and around in his head. *Strange now to think of you, gone.* He's setting the poem to music. It's so comforting, so distracting. It's really fun. His arm is still bandaged, but he can hold the guitar, play chords. And he can use the laptop with one hand.

He's trying to imagine things from Claire's point of view. How must it feel to have her father estranged, dying? She hasn't visited him yet. Yossi can't believe it. He knows how difficult her childhood was but this breaks some boundary. Respect for the weak and the sick, and respect for parents, aren't these bottom lines? Some things are just wrong. Such as attacking an old man. Claire's always telling him these violent criminals have awful childhoods. That's wrong of their parents but still, an old man!

Disrespecting the dead is the same. Intuitively, universally, wrong. Why is she being like this? He plays the chorus again.

"Yoss?" Roimata stands at the door of his study. "Can I come in?"

"Sure." He puts aside the paper he's been scribbling on. Turns his chair from the desk and starts to play his guitar. They do a mean version of *Wild Horses* together and he starts to play that.

"What's that you were playing? You writing a song? Can I hear it?"

"I'm just experimenting with something. It's nowhere near ready for anyone to hear." He starts to sing, and nods at her to join in.

"Please. I want to hear your song."

"Ok, but it's embarrassing."

He sings it through once, stumbling a bit, experimenting with the key.

"Play it again."

This time, when he gets to the line about Ray Charles, Roi joins in, doing an amazing bluesy-gospel riff on the word *suffer*, as a background to his singing. Wow.

Yossi has tears in his eyes.

"It's about Patrick, isn't it?"

"It's a poem a poet called Allen Ginsberg wrote when his mother died. I think she had a mental illness."

"What's kaddish?"

Guilt attack. His daughter is fifteen and she doesn't know what kaddish is. His parents must be turning in their graves. But she's not Jewish. Her mother's not Jewish. Would his parents have loved them? He knows they would have.

"It's our prayers for the dead. The Jewish way of mourning."

"Say a bit."

He does.

"You could take that and put it in the song. Loop it. Can I add some violin?"

They spend the next few hours tinkering, composing, singing, then stop for iced tea and fixes of biscotti. Roi records him saying kaddish and samples it. It never fails to send shivers up and down his spine. Never fails to make him miss his mother and his father, think about his grandparents. He shudders at the thought that recording it like this may be disrespectful. It contains the word God but, hey, it's just a word, and it's only for them.

"Why would you go on and on about the glory of God when someone has died?" she asks when he translates a bit of the kaddish for her.

"That's a very tricky question. Religion's one of those things where you have to, *like*," – he does an exaggerated parody of her generation's fondness for that word – "*like*, be there. Do you wish we'd raised you in a religion?"

"How can I know?" Roimata says. "Do you believe in anything? I mean, not God, but anything?" She asks casually, as though she is asking whether he would like a cup of tea.

"I definitely believe in evolution. As far as morals go, I believe in the golden rule, you know, Do Unto Others. Religion can be a force for good. It gives people comfort." Yossi is struggling. He wishes Claire were here.

"Are you glad you were brought up Jewish?"

"Absolutely. My parents weren't particularly religious, but there are lovely rituals, a great culture. Are we depriving you of that?"

She shrugs.

"It's the supernatural things your mother and I have a problem with. It's not that things aren't amazing. I can't think of anything more wonderful than evolution. It's just that, although there's a lot we don't know yet, we do believe it's all knowable. There's no great mystery, just complexity. Does that make sense?"

"It's awful to think Granddad will die. But I hardly know him."

"When my mother died I went to synagogue a lot. I really wanted to believe that I would see her again."

"Is Mum grieving?"

"Of course."

"How can we help her?"

"You help her every day. You are the best thing in her life."

"Hey, why don't we put in a break with a klezmer feel?" She picks up her violin.

Kids have that amazing ability to skip from the big questions of life to what they are doing in that moment, effortlessly and with equal concentration. She's still a kid then. What can they tell her? How can they help her get through this? Life is weird.

"Yossi?"

What now?

"In that poem, why does he miss her corsets and her eyes?"

"I'm thinking those are the two things he remembers really

strongly. Corsets are about restraints and looking right. She might not miss those. And eyes are about perception. Experiencing stuff. She might miss that."

"What I would miss about you," she says, smiling, "is this delicious biscotti."

She's ok then.

He'll watch her but she's ok. Her joke is so like something Claire would have said when they were getting too deep, too cheesy. It's Claire he needs to worry about.

36

THE NEXT NIGHT, CLAIRE'S READING the latest *Medical Journal* in bed. There's a story about the actual physical changes in the brains of abused children. The way experience imprints viscerally on brains, early, before conscious memory kicks in. Che's six already; a lot of damage may have been done. They need to act as soon as they can.

The phone rings. It's her best surgical registrar, Angel, a serious Chinese girl. Bright as a button. Claire starts getting dressed. She knows Angel would not call her unless it was necessary.

"Triumph Wharerau. Hypotensive. Temp 40. Distended abdomen. Tachychardic. No bowel sounds."

Shit. She knew he was brewing something. He's in septic shock. Peritonitis. She throws on track pants and a sweatshirt, working the clothes around the phone.

Angel sounds well aware of how sick he is, and that it should have been picked up earlier.

"I'm on my way."

Jesus, this has happened fast. She'd checked on him only this afternoon. Now he's gravely ill. As she drives, she visualises little Triumph, going over and over her examination of him that afternoon. Nothing. She starts to think through the operation she will do. Peritoneal infection: repair, purge, decompress, control. Aggressive debridement, as she was trained to do, is now controversial. She'll see what she finds when she gets in there. She thinks about Patch, already beaten down by life. Repair, purge, decompress, control. She will not let him die.

Triumph's in the ICU, nasal prongs helping him breathe, tubes pumping replacement fluids and blunderbuss antibiotics. She checks his ECG monitor and oxygen sats. He's a sick little mite. She talks to the intensivist in charge.

Claire finds Patch outside standing in the still-warm air, smoking. The Sky Tower, lit red, rises up above the carpark building like one of the machines in *War of the Worlds*. The hospital's deserted.

"He's really sick. I'm sorry. It's probably what we call adhesions, like scar tissue that forms and blocks things up. It's likely his bowel has stopped working and then split. Then his poo has probably leaked into his tummy and caused an infection. I'll need to operate. But first we have to treat him for septic shock. His body's gone into emergency mode. His blood pressure's very low, which makes his heart work faster to try to push blood around."

As she heads back to the ICU Patch walks beside her with her knock-kneed gait. There's the bit Claire hasn't said. The bit that would only terrify Patch. The delicate balance of the next few hours. The intensivist's job is to get him well enough to cope, keep him alive, get him out of shock; her job, as a surgeon, to go in, intervene, get rid of the toxic bag of pus in the boy's body. Too early and the operation might kill him. Too late and the infection might kill him. This is a judgement call. She can feel her adrenaline pumping.

They decide he's well enough at five-thirty in the morning. The anaesthetist is tall and he sets the table high in the hushed theatre. She can do this.

"Bloody gang parents. Did you see the father? He stinks. There'll be trouble if this kid dies," says one of the nurses.

"The poor wee fellow," says another.

Triumph's pale and cold. There are several scars on his huge bloated belly, one angry red from her operation last week. Did she cause this?

She's in. Repair, purge, decompress, control.

Afterwards, she's bone-weary but wide awake. The vivid blue ICU is stuffy, brightly lit, and noisy with beeping and alarms twenty-four hours a day. At least the phone's quiet at night. Each patient has one dedicated nurse and tonight a bubbly Australian girl, who's overdone the fake tan, is keeping Triumph alive. She's wearing scrubs decorated with blue and red teddy bears, a stethoscope covered in a giraffe soft toy slung over her shoulder.

Triumph is intubated. He's naked, sprawled on his back, puffy against the *SpongeBob* sheets, his genitals bruised and swollen, a bandage covering the new wound. The usual array of tubes and catheters and electrodes snake over his small body again. Claire can't help herself, checking each one. Patch sleeps in a La-Z-Boy beside the high bed.

After covering Triumph and giving surgical orders to the nurse, Claire heads to the waiting room. There he is, Knockers, slumped on a puke-green plastic chair, his biker boots up on another, staring at the TV, where a nerdy white preacher peddles salvation. She makes him a sweet, milky coffee and sits down beside him. She hands him the polystyrene cup. He continues to stare at the TV, no acknowledgement, and no eye contact.

She tells him what she did in the surgery, that they will need to watch Triumph for twenty-four hours.

"He's sick, really sick, but if we get him through tonight, we'll have much more of an idea. The doctors in there are good at dealing with any crisis he might have and he has his own nurse watching him all night."

He doesn't look at her.

She's home early in the morning just long enough to shower and change her clothes. Her limbs feel heavy.

Yossi follows her to her car.

"Claire, your Dad. They're saying he mightn't recover. Could you visit him?"

"No."

"He's dying, Mum. He's DYING," Roimata shouts from the door.

Claire hadn't noticed her follow them out.

"Look, Roi, I'm sorry about my family. But there are worse

things in life. You're loved, protected, fed. Stop being so bloody ungrateful."

"I hate you. He's your father!"

Patch is there with Triumph, as always, wearing her ancient woolly hat and the same pilled red jersey and black track pants she was wearing last night. The only clothes Claire's ever seen her in.

"Knockers was like, whoa, you came out in the middle of the night to save him," she says. "He wants to call this one in here Star, after the Starship Hospital, if it's a girl."

Claire smiles and puts her arm around Patch, giving her a light squeeze. Patch jumps slightly, tenses up. As Claire turns to go, Patch looks around and leans in close.

"Knockers, he wants to know, you know Patrick Bowerman, the guy done for, like, that hitchhiker girl. Was he your father?" she asks.

Claire just nods. She's too tired to care. What will notoriety mean? More respect in their strange survivalist world?

Patch swallows, her brown eyes darting all around the unit. She almost whispers. "Knockers, he reckons some of the old guys in the gang say your Dad never did it. They say he took the rap. They looked after him in jail." Patch leans over Triumph and strokes his cheek as though she's never spoken.

It's hot in the ICU and Claire's sweating and dizzy. Why can't everyone just leave it alone? She doesn't want to think about it ever again. Everyone's on a mission to make her think he's innocent. Poor Dad. She feels a wave of horror. She's heard he's innocent, he's guilty, he's innocent so many times before. She needs to stay strong, not think about the past. She's late for rounds.

When Claire gets home that night, Yossi and Roimata are not there. Yossi texts to let her know they are at the hospital sitting with Patrick. Roimata texts to ask her to come. She doesn't reply. She pours herself a glass of wine and curls up on the couch with a couple of chocolate biscuits. Watches Mad Men. They're still not home at ten thirty when she goes to bed.

37

HER ALARM WAKES HER AT six. She has to do a difficult operation today.

Opening the door to Roimata's room, she sees her daughter fast asleep, curled on her side. Yossi is in the spare room and he doesn't stir when she peers around the door.

She'd forgotten how tropical Auckland can feel. Her clothes crackle in the uneasy stillness. People in the hospital grounds take shelter in shadows. Up on the surgical floor, she crosses the ward to pull the curtains, protecting her sick patients from the harsh glare. The city and the harbour stretch out before her, the Fullers ferry gliding across glassy water, swiftly passing a huge container ship. There are few small craft around today, forecasters warning of a cyclone heading their way. Fiji's been devastated by the storm overnight.

Her phone beeps and it's a text from Yossi. *We won't be going to Waiheke. Visit Patrick tonight?*

The islands in the inner harbour look close and detailed. She can see trees on Motutapu. Waiheke's a blue shape in the distance. For the first time she's not looking forward to their weekend there. She shuts out the harbour and the brightness with faded curtains that are covered in smiley faces.

She stretches her neck and shoulders on her way out of the room. The girl she's about to operate on is medically fragile. They all wonder whether they shouldn't just be leaving her to die in peace. Whose call is it? Her parents have consented. They've all agreed to go ahead.

She texts Yossi back. *I still want to go to Waiheke. I rang ICU. No change in Patrick.*

It's good to get into the air-conditioned theatre, away from patients and patients' families. She pauses for a moment and checks everyone's ready. Sophie is on the table, masked, intubated, unconscious. Lines and tape jostle for space on her bony chest. She cuts into the belly, and identifies the tumour quickly. Then the beeps start.

"Right, hold on for a minute, please," says the anaesthetist, taking over and giving orders.

Claire stands out of the way, holding her gloved hands in front of her. She motions to a nurse to turn off the Radiohead that's been blaring. There's a nightmare then. Lots of beeping, watching the anaesthetist give CPR, doing compressions herself for a time, and eventually, the giving up. They're all quiet for a minute, looking at each other, knowing they have to let her go.

The anaesthetist pronounces the girl dead, and then asks them to leave everything as it is because it will be a coroner's case.

Claire stretches her arms and shoulders. Tries to relax herself. This is awful. So sad.

Sam, who'd asked her to remove the tumour, comes rushing in just as they all turn away and take off their gloves.

"What –?"

"Gone. I'm so sorry, Sam."

"Ok."

They'd all known this was on the cards; this child had been through so much.

"Shall I come with you to tell the parents?" she asks Sam. "It's better to have someone who was actually in here and I will want talk to them anyway."

"You know what, I think she was only holding on for her parents' sake." Sam sighs heavily.

Claire takes his arm and guides him through the door.

"They're at the PICU. In different rooms."

Oh Jesus, she'd forgotten. This is the difficult divorce case the team had discussed at their weekly meeting. It's World War Three.

Both Mum and Dad had applied to police to have the other banned from the hospital. Neither succeeded. Great.

On the way down, she checks her phone. A flurry of missed texts.
From Yossi. *We shouldn't go to Waiheke. Storm brewing and your father very sick.* Then – *Roimata refusing to go to W.*
From Roimata. *I'm staying at Charlotte's if you go.*
From Debs, a missed call and then a text. *I couldn't get you. Happy to have Roi. She's here already. Hope that's ok.*

As they walk into the PICU area, Claire glances into the nurses' tearoom where Sophie's Mum sits clutching the necklace that nurses give child cancer patients, one bead for each procedure. Claire's teeth clench hard and she catches her breath, knowing the impact of the news that she must break to this mother. She beckons the charge nurse, tells her to fetch Dad into the tearoom immediately.

"Do you want to do the talking?" she asks Sam.
"I could go to Dad, you tell Mum?"
"No. We've got to tell them together."
"Ok. You, then."
Sam looks devastated.
They wait outside the tearoom, out of Mum's sight, until the nurse brings Dad, hand firmly on his arm. They walk in after him. Mum stands. Claire has one last glance at the notes in her hand, checking the names. Oh God, their faces are willing her to say something else, not what she has to say.
"David, Annette, I'm sorry to tell you that Sophie died in the operation."
She pauses as Mum cries out and sinks back down onto the couch. Dad turns and leans on the wall.
"Her heart gave up. We tried everything we could to get it going again but it wouldn't. She was anaesthetised at the time and wouldn't have felt any pain." She pauses and they are both silent.
"Now, I'm going to leave you with Sam. I know you are shocked right now but if you have any questions later, I'm here in the

hospital for the rest of the day so ask Anna to get me. I'm so sorry. Sophie was a beautiful wee girl."

With that, Claire leaves. But she hears the arguing and the blaming start up behind her. Poor Sam. Those poor parents. That poor little girl.

She calls Yossi on her way to get changed.

"You need to visit your father, Claire. What's going on?"

"I will. I just need some time." She's exhausted. She wants to explain things to Roimata. She wants a moment to think.

"Roi's very upset with you, Claire. She's going to stay the weekend with Debs. Debs wants to visit your Dad too, so she's happy to get her to the hospital."

Oh God. This is getting more and more out of control. It's as though tentacles are reaching out to them all from her past, dragging them back into that dark crevasse, her life before she left New Zealand. She needs to protect Roimata from all this.

"You didn't ask me."

"You were in surgery. You didn't answer. I had to make a decision. She's freaking out, Claire. Just go and see him. You'll feel better."

"I'm going to Waiheke. I think you and Roimata should come as well."

She jumps into the tiled shower and rubs shampoo into her hair, the citrus fragrance astringent and cleansing. She turns the mixer until the water's almost scalding. She leans her head right back, water streaming down her face. Separating out hanks of hair with her fingers she rinses out the shampoo, pulling on her hair so hard she almost tugs it out of her scalp. The harder she tugs, the better it feels.

The rest of the team is heading to Newmarket for a rare Friday drink, needing to debrief after Sophie's death and the horrible family tension around it. Claire can't face it. She needs to hold herself together. She's desperate to see Roimata, hold her, comfort her.

She only just makes the six o'clock ferry. People are filing off the boat, dressed up for their night out in Auckland. Yossi hasn't joined the queue to board, he's waiting nearby for her. He takes her bag from her and puts it down on the ground.

"Claire, I don't think we should go. The weather is terrible. We need to visit Patrick. He's really sick. Let's just go home. We can go next weekend."

"I need a bit of time. I love it at Waiheke."

"I don't want you to go on your own again. I'll come with you. But I don't like it."

The wind has been getting up for some time and now it starts to rain. People squeal and jog up the gangplank. Claire sits at a table beside the window as usual. Yossi sits in one of the centre seats and takes out his book. Could he be sulking? She has never known him sulk. It's not his style. She moves over to be with him and he does not look up. Claire leans back and closes her eyes.

She remembers Sophie's slight body and all the things wrong with it. She remembers the mother's sparkly wrap-around bangle and the scars from long-ago acne on her cheeks. The father's girlfriend, dressed up to the nines in high wedge shoes and a skimpy dress, had stayed out of the meeting. Thank God. Imagine if Dad had insisted on having her there. There'd been all sorts of trouble with them during the treatment. Sam had hated dealing with them, she knew, because of the effect on Sophie.

What if Patrick dies while she is in Waiheke and Roimata is there in Auckland? Oh my God, she feels sick. She doesn't want Roi to have to take responsibility for this. If only Yossi had made Roimata come too. She'll ring Debs as soon as they get there and talk to her about not letting Roimata take it all on board too much.

They suit up in wet weather gear for the trip in the tinny around the headland to Ruby Bay. The wind's angry now; it whips their hair into their faces and makes the rain sting their hands. It's actually lovely, exhilarating.

They don't talk as they make several trips from the boat to the bach, unloading gear. The wind is loud. The native flaxes and coprosma they have planted along their path dance wildly in the wind. Yossi heads back outside even though they have got everything. He must be going to check the boat is secure. She sees him pause in the garden, checking on the plants, his jacket flapping.

She sends a text to Roimata. *I miss you already. Please take care.* There's no reply. She should be there with her.

There are several bags of shopping Yossi has dumped on the bench. Claire unpacks them. She chops cauliflower and puts it on to steam. Starts to panfry snapper, just dipping it in a little egg and flour first. When Yossi comes in she hands him a wine. They clink glasses from habit, then sink into the armchairs facing the boiling bay.

"I would have cooked. I was going to roast the cauliflower." Yossi comes in to the kitchen. "I told you I had planned a lovely dinner."

"No you didn't."

"I did actually. You were totally distracted."

He's so anal sometimes. God forbid they might have to eat something plain and not gourmet. The lights flicker and go out. The oven makes a strange peep.

"Shit, it might be a power cut," says Claire. She tries a light switch. Nothing.

Claire goes to the cupboard and gets two torches and the first aid kit. Both torches go. She puts them on the table, just as her father used to do. What else? Her Dad always had a transistor radio. She hopes Yossi's iPad is charged, because hers isn't.

"What about dinner?"

"It's almost ready. I'll leave it in the pan a few more minutes, and it will keep cooking. We'll just make a salad if it doesn't."

Rain hoses at the window under pressure, wind keening. As the last light fades Claire finds a box of taper candles in a kitchen drawer. Patrick has written something on the packet. Such familiar writing. Claire peers at the faded letters. *NB Emergency kit with gas lamp in high cupboard in laundry.* She takes it to show Yossi.

"We should go back, Claire. To Roi. And Patrick. This weather. We shouldn't have come." He pauses for a minute and clicks his phone a few times. "Oh shit. The ferries are cancelled." He stands and stares out the window.

She grabs a torch and a coat and goes into the storm. The wind pushes her back. She directs the torch down at her feet as she picks her way down the wooden stairs, slick with water, to the basement. In the musty laundry, she finds a cardboard box labelled EMERGENCY in the same bold hand. There's a box of Meccano tucked in there. He must have put that there for her in case they had a long night and she needed distraction. Not a doll or a teddy bear. He was cool like that.

A gasp escapes her. Dad, she thinks. He's dying.

Yossi grates Parmesan onto their cauliflower and squeezes lemon onto their fish. Claire can't really taste anything. Eating by candlelight in front of the huge windows, they're floating above the sea. The lights of the city have disappeared and there are no boats in the bay. The storm is so loud they can hardly hear each other.

"Brent said Māori believe that when people die their spirits journey up to the top of New Zealand, where they leap off into the other world," Yossi says.

"It's a lovely myth," Claire says.

Yossi frowns.

"Did you get to come here much when you were a child?"

"Only a few times. Mum hated it here. It was too dark and too isolated. She was afraid here."

"Did you visit your Dad when he was in jail?"

"I did, yeah." Claire gets up, starts packing up the plates. Bright lightning flashes, then thunder. The rain's even heavier; she can't hear herself think. She moves over to the kitchen and piles the plates into the sink.

"What was that like?"

Claire opens the freezer. "We better eat some ice-cream, in case the freezer defrosts." She begins to hull strawberries.

"You should talk to Roimata about it. Answer her questions. She wants to know," Yossi says.

"She's so young. I don't want her to think about such things. I want her to have a childhood. Life will get tough soon enough."

"She's fifteen, Claire. You can't protect her forever."

There's no music while they eat their desserts and then clean up, this silence unusual for their household. Claire moves two chairs close together and puts a lit candle on a little table. The area glows and flickers, separating itself off in the candle light like a confessional. She sinks into one of the chairs, curls her legs up under herself.

"Your Dad was pardoned, right? What happened to him then?" Yossi asks her.

Obviously this is not going to go away.

"He came home to live with us. For a while. But they argued. My mum believed he was guilty, so they split up."

"What was it like when he got arrested?"

Her father, hiding his face with a green jersey as he got in the police car. The dark patch on the front of his trousers where he'd wet himself. Her mother screaming. The neighbour had given Claire a packet of Sparkles and put her to bed. She'd found a purple one sticky on her pillow the next morning and had put it back in her mouth even though it had fluff on it.

"I was only five, Yossi."

"Claire, you can't just pretend this is not happening. You'll feel much better if you visit your father."

"I will. When I'm ready."

"Why do you feel such anger at him? He is dying, Claire. A sick elderly man, dying alone."

"I don't want that man in my life. Or yours. Or Roimata's. All he does is let people down and use people and hurt people. Some relationships are just broken, there's no point flogging them. Can't you trust me?"

"Claire, you've never told me how your mother died," he says.

Why doesn't he listen?

"Yossi, I'm really tired. I don't want to talk about it." She takes a torch and goes to bed. In spite of the weight in her heart, it's actually nice in bed, snuggled up with the storm raging around her. When Yossi comes to bed she pretends to be asleep. The rain hisses; every door and window seems to be rattling in the wind. She's never talked to anyone about what happened with her mother. There's no point in starting now. What does he want her to say?

She remembers her joy at opening the letter offering a surgical internship at Great Ormond Street. The first person she'd told was her mother.

"I'll be all alone."

"Mum, it's the best children's hospital in the world."

"I'll just have to die, then. Get out of your way."

Claire had heard it all before so many times.

"Mum, promise me you won't hurt yourself."

"Everyone would be better off without me."

"We'll think of something. Perhaps you can come and live in London with me. Just promise me you won't hurt yourself."

"Off you go. I'll be all right."

Rita killed herself a week before the date on Claire's ticket out, in glorious theatrical fashion, drinking a bottle of Remy Martin neat and taking a box of aspirin. She meant it, then, not like the other times. Claire hadn't got an answer to her phone calls, had driven late at night and found her. She called the police, cleaned up, identified the body at the morgue. She cried only twice, first when someone handed her a brown paper bag. In it, the clothes her mother had been wearing. Her cheap, plastic-strapped watch. Then, when she had to iron some clothes for the funeral director to dress the body in. She'd ironed the blue linen dress her mother had loved, working out every wrinkle, weeping.

She'd organised a funeral. Her father hadn't come. He was drunk every day anyway. He slurred his words as he spoke too loudly to Claire about his regrets. He had failed Rita.

Claire hadn't known what she'd felt. Numb. Short of breath. Fragile. As she'd flown out of New Zealand, a sense that she could at last start living her life.

Her mother had warned her. It was her fault. She had failed her mother.

She gets up while it's still dark, creeps out into the living room and sits on the window seat, watching raindrops land and drip and merge. Deal with it, she tells herself. And for Roi's sake, at the moment, that means visiting Patrick. She can't protect Roi from this so she must be a role model. Be calm. She counts the seconds between the flashes of lightning and the rumble of thunder, as her Dad taught her to do. The gaps are longer and longer. She sits and watches the trees as the wind quietens. Be strong. Be kind.

38

ON THE WAY HOME FROM the ferry, they stop at the hospital. Claire scrabbles around and finds a grubby comb. She runs it through her hair and, looking in the rear vision mirror, pushes it all up into a clip again. He last saw her as a very young woman. Now, she's a middle-aged surgeon, the mother of a fifteen-year-old, with lines and wrinkles. He's in a coma, in Critical Care. He won't be able to look at her.

When she climbs out, Yossi takes her hand. He's salty and sweaty from their weekend. He starts to move off towards the main building. She stops him, takes her hand out of his, looks at his intelligent face.

"Yoss, I –"

"I know. We need to talk. Let's just do this first."

Yossi goes through the door of Critical Care but Claire pauses. It will be ok.

She hasn't been in here before. A standard intensive care unit, open plan, with subdued lighting, no windows and a lot of technology. Yossi is standing beside a bed. She walks across, careful not to look at others, aware of the intense curiosity that many visitors show. Some patients lie naked, in order to be observed all the time. Everyone here has a terrible story, she thinks. Mine is nothing.

Roimata's in a vinyl armchair, leaving the straight-backed chair beside the bed for Claire. Her face lights up.

"Look, it's my Mum. It's your daughter Claire. She's come to see you." Then she whispers to Claire and Yossi. "They said he's still not really talking."

How could Yossi allow Roimata to be exposed to all this? This is exactly the kind of thing Claire had been trying to protect her from. She touches Roi's arm and kisses her on the head on her way past.

She looks along the shrunken arm to the face. It's strained, bruised and swollen, but it is her father. His head has been shaved and there is an ugly line of stitches. He stirs just a little, maybe, though his eyes stay closed. She steps forward and puts a hand on the blankets lightly.

"Hi Dad. You don't look too well."

Patrick screws up his face like a child, and plucks at his IV. She gestures for Roimata to hand her his chart from the end of the bed. He's head-injured and traumatised from the attack, in withdrawal from alcohol, and emphysemic after years of smoking. He's on a lot of pain medication. He won't come back from this. If the head injury doesn't kill him, an infection will. His immune system must be so weakened. He'll be moved into hospice care if he lives much longer. A cold sadness engulfs her.

"Dad. I'm here." She bends down and brushes her cheek against his soft cheek. There is no response. He looks fragile.

"Sit down, Claire. Hold his hand," Yossi says. His voice comes from far away. But she does sit down and she takes an emaciated hand, which feels dry and papery. Patrick has quieted a bit. His eyes are still closed.

"Talk to him, Mum," Roimata says.

God, talk to him. She may still be able to give an old man some comfort. She must set an example, for Roimata.

"We love Waiheke, Dad," she says. "We go every weekend. It's looking great. The Island has really changed but our bay hasn't changed much."

No flicker of response.

"Our happiest times were at Waiheke," she says to Roimata. "Dad and me, I mean. Mum hated it, even though it was her bach from her family."

"I love it too," Roimata says to the old man. "I really miss London, but the bach is the best thing about Auckland."

There is quiet for a while.

"I wish I'd known you. I bet you're stubborn and strong like my Mum," Roimata says.

Yossi laughs.

"Me? Stubborn?" Claire laughs too.

The man in the bed is still. Claire strokes his cheek.

"What was he like when you met him?" She's not sure whether she's asking Roi or Yossi.

"He talked a bit like you," Roimata says, "the same accent and the way you say things."

Really? Claire had no idea.

When they'd first moved back here, Claire had made a few phone-calls. She'd known he was still drinking, living in a boarding house, often in minor trouble with the police. The last time she'd seen him was seventeen years ago, just days after her mother had died, at a flat he'd rented in Māngere. A row of state houses with bare, neglected gardens. Swathes of ripped fabric and lace glared from filthy windows. A pile of discarded bottles leaned against a little stone wall. Her father had looked absolutely dreadful. Baggy track pants on his skinny legs and a huge pot belly straining against a singlet. *Hi Dad. I'm off to live in London next week and I thought I should come and say goodbye.*

Slurring his words, though it was only late morning, he had sought her advice about a rash on his stomach, asked for money and boasted about his travel to London thirty years earlier. She got his television and video working for him. She remembers driving away, crying. Listening to music – she can't remember what it was – on her car stereo. Turning it up so loud that it hurt her ears.

She wanted to check with Yossi how difficult Patrick had been when they had met him, and how Roimata had taken it, what she had seen. But this wasn't the time. She should have asked while they were at Waiheke, but she'd been so angry. Patrick may be able to hear everything they say.

"I hope you realized what a lovely granddaughter you have, Dad," she says to Patrick, taking his hand again. "You'd be so proud of her. I'm glad you got to meet her. And her father, Yossi, who is lovely."

"I'd like to talk to Simon Flaxstone," Roimata says. "He's interviewed Patrick. Maybe he can tell us more about him and what happened."

Roi has no idea. She thinks it will be black and white, assumes he will be innocent. She doesn't know how hard Claire has worked to leave it all behind.

It wasn't easy, the moving to London. She'd written to her father in the first few years, had never received a reply. She'd rung him twice and both times he'd asked her to send money. She'd written when Roimata was born, and sent him a photo. No reply. She'd grieved so much for her mother. Selfishly wanted to share Roimata with someone else who would feel that surge of animal love for her, as surely a grandmother would. She'd thought a lot about her unconditional love for her baby, tried to understand that her parents must have felt the same about her. She'd imagined her mother's voice saying, *Well, not so perfect now, are you, Miss High-and-Mighty, a single mother.* Was that unfair? Whatever else, her mother would have been terrified for the safety of Roimata. Her love had been spent protecting Claire from imaginary foes, from all the awful people in the world plotting to get them. Once she had a child to shelter, Claire understood how much of her mother's energy that took.

Patrick's eyelids flutter but she knows it's nothing. She tells Roimata about him being funny. The way he would sing musical comedy like *The Mikado,* and act all silly and make Claire and her mother laugh.

She sings softly to him, *Blue Moon,* leaning in close to his head, her hand stroking his arm. It had been his favourite song. Patrick lies still and remote. She watches his chest rising and falling.

Then she has had enough.

She gets up to go, but Roimata and Yossi don't want to leave him.

"You need to think of the other patients, and he needs to rest," Claire says.

"I don't want to leave him alone," Yossi says.

"We'll be really quiet," whispers Roi.

"I have to go and see a patient," Claire says. "Then we'll go home."

She sits on a bench seat outside Emergency. She'd tried to work out years ago whether he was guilty or not. She'd talked to his lawyers, read newspapers, asked questions. There'd been endless discussion about it among adults around her for her entire childhood. She'd lived through so many trials and appeals that she can no longer remember one from another. In the end, she'd decided to move on. There are things that she will just never know and she has learned to live with that. Still, enormous guilt hits her that she couldn't help her father live a better life. He is dying now.

She wants to leave it all and go back to London.

She doesn't look up at the hospital as she threads through the narrow pathway to Starship. Work will make her feel better.

Logging on to the computer, she looks through her list for tomorrow. She asks the Charge Nurse what has happened about Che MacKenzie's care.

"I'm not sure. He's been on his own since I've been on."

Patch is beside Triumph. Both are asleep. In the bed opposite Che lies watching The Simpsons with the sound muted. It's late; he should be asleep too. He's in a singlet and boxers. His little body, still bruised in places, is solid and his cheeks are chubby. His teeth are terrible and she makes a note to get a dentist to check him before he leaves the hospital. She'll check his ears, too. He probably has glue ear, because he isn't hearing that well. She wants to know whether he's been immunised, especially against meningitis.

It's airless and he has a crumpled cream sheet half over him, his feet sticking out. Claire pulls the curtains around Che. He's not sad, but he's dissociated. He's too passive. He doesn't say a word. He's clutching something under the sheet. She gently draws his arm out and it's a New World bag.

"Can I look in here?" she whispers.

He nods.

A singlet and some spare undies. The bear that a hospital sponsor gives each child. A toothbrush set, a useless disposable one. It looks as though he's been using it for some time.

Claire stays with Che until he falls asleep. He looks angelic. If he'd died from these injuries, the country would have been in an uproar. Like the baby from Whanganui that died a few weeks ago. The ubiquitous photo of the wee girl in a pink woolly hat, out of focus, taken by God knows who, has become a symbol of innocence and of the depravity of the family she was born into.

But if he survives and grows up damaged, like Patch and Knockers have, he will become the target of hatred and mistrust.

Around two o'clock in the morning she calls Yossi.

"Roimata's fallen asleep," he tells her.

"I think you should wake her up. Please can we all go home now? I'll meet you at the car. It'll be too hard for me to get through security and I don't want to disturb the staff and patients at this time of night."

"Claire, you can sit with him now, and I'll take Roimata home, if you like," Yossi says.

Probably a good idea, but she needs to be careful. Although she feels ok, there is a deep sadness pushing down into her body. It won't help anyone if she loses it. She's still got the Peteru case hanging over her, and a lot of other cases.

"No," she says. "I'm glad I saw him, but I want to go home now."

Yossi drives through the empty streets.

Claire tries to hug and kiss Roi good night but Roi shrugs her off. What do they want from her? Do they want her to break down, not cope?

39

CLAIRE CREEPS OUT OF BED, dresses quietly and goes into Roimata's room, which is stuffy and untidy, her clothes from last night dropped beside the bed. She kisses Roi on her head gently, and says in a low voice, "Roi Roi-bird, wake up. It's time to go to school."

Roimata groans. "Can I have the day off? I want to sleep."

"No. I'll drop you at school, though, since you had such a late night."

Roimata is still sulky on the trip. There's not much point in trying to talk to her when she's so tired, and Claire needs to concentrate on the traffic as they crawl along congested Gillies Ave.

When she sneaks in ten minutes late to a ward meeting, the nurses are complaining about the behaviour of Che's stepfather, the thin pale man Claire had disliked on sight.

"Mum's only been with him for a couple of months."

"Is he a stepfather? Does he have any rights?" someone asks.

Claire's under pressure to discharge Che, who is not sick enough to be in hospital, certainly not in a surgical bed. Her head of department has told her to leave it to the social workers, to get him out of the ward as soon as possible.

"We need to sort where he's going to go," she says to the social worker, Lata, who's middle-aged and refreshingly pragmatic. "Do you think Heaven beats him too?"

"On the record, we don't know. It's difficult to find out. Off the record, she doesn't give a toss, certainly wouldn't let concern for Che get in the way of a relationship with any man that'll look at her," Lata says.

"So the earlier beatings?"

"My guess – other boyfriends."

"Ok, well we'll have to discharge him very soon. Can you get back to me about the plans for him? Oh, and if the so-called stepfather comes in, Janet, can you let me know? I'll have a word to him about his behaviour." Claire finishes off the meeting.

"I want the police involved. If someone doesn't call CYF, I will," she says to Lata privately, on the way out of the room.

"I'm onto it," Lata says. "That man is not taking him home."

Some sanity.

At eleven o'clock Claire has a moment to feel tired after being up most of the night. She sits down at her desk and straight away Janet, the darling, brings her a takeaway coffee and hurries out of the office. The bitter creaminess of the coffee is reviving.

She thinks of her father, in hospital, so skinny and quiet. She'd rung first thing this morning and the geriatrician had said he thought there wasn't long to go. She thinks of Roimata up there in the hospital last night, so certain, so unafraid. Of Yossi and how he doesn't understand her at all. How coming back here has driven them apart, as she had feared it would.

There's a message to ring Sam. She'd had a message from him earlier letting her know that the CEO had handed the case over to CYF and the police were to be involved. The media has been full of it. She dials Sam.

"Claire, the Peterus have agreed to meet with me. Just me. One last chance to talk them into it. Tonight."

"Sam, that's great. Well done."

"A TV reporter's been trying to arrange a meeting between me and the family, so they can film it," Sam says. "No way I'm letting them film the meeting. But I've agreed to talk to them afterwards."

Thank God. Sensible Sam. No doubt they'll make that refusal look arrogant, but there's no way that can work out. The pressure of the camera would simply change everything. It's just too delicate.

The Peterus must be thinking a media crusade will protect them from the evil forces.

"Good on you. So now what?"

"Isa'ako and Kate have agreed to meet with me tonight, as long as the cameras can film me going in to the meeting, and coming out, they'll talk with me off camera. Can I meet with you first, to go over what to say?"

"Won't I just make things worse? I'm a surgeon, Sam. Bloody hopeless at the touchy-feely stuff."

They both laugh at the stereotype.

"Claire, you're so kind. You don't fool me. Your patients know you are on their side, even when you act all prickly."

Really? She's not so sure.

Janet's back, grimacing a little and gesturing at the ward with her thumb.

"Sam, I'll have to go. I'll think about it. Does it have to be tonight?"

"Yes, the deadline they've been given by CYFS is tomorrow. Our last chance to avoid the horrible legal stuff."

"OK, well, I'll text you soon and suggest a time."

She hangs up and switches her attention immediately to Janet.

"Sorry, darling, but that charming man's here," Janet says.

"Who?"

"The evil stepfather. Heaven's bloke. He's causing trouble. But drink your coffee first, for God's sake."

Claire gulps down the hot coffee. She almost regurgitates it when she gets close to the room. She can smell his BO from the doorway. She knows he's high as soon as she sets eyes on him. Pacing up and down the length of the room, a hip-jerking walk, threat in every muscle. Muttering. *Fuck* every second word. His sunken eyes move a lot. Crystal meth. 'P' they call it here. Not that she's an expert, but she's seen its effects among the young parents at Great Ormond Street.

Heaven is whining to a nurse. Che's well enough to come home now and it's a real trek for them to come in from Swanson. Can she get some petrol money?

Che's just listening, his head down, his face unreadable. Claire stays out of it at first, stopping beside Triumph in the bed opposite and looking at his charts, listening, observing.

The nurse jumps and drops a chart with a clatter when Jayson interrupts Heaven and yells at the room.

"We're fuckin' taking him home. You can't fuckin' keep him here. He's our kid."

Patch and Knockers have both been sitting beside Triumph's bed, looking down. Now Patch walks slowly over and sits beside Che, who's playing with his game again. She places one hand on his arm and her other on his head, leaning awkwardly to put herself between the boy and the man.

Claire takes control.

"Hello." She holds her hand out to the man, who doesn't take it. "I'm Claire Bowerman, one of the doctors here. I met you the other day. Is there a problem?"

"Yes there's a fuckin' problem. You cunts won't let us take the kid home. Yes I have a fuckin' problem with that."

"Sir, would you please come and talk about this in my office. It's not appropriate in this room. There are sick children here. And watch your language please."

"Yeah, sure, so you can steal the fuckin' boy while you fuckin' have me out of here. I'm not fuckin' stupid."

"Have you notified Security? And Social Work?" Claire asks the nurse.

"Yes, they're on their way."

"Sir, you have to calm down and come and talk with me."

"Hey, you're the fuckin' cow that's trying to take that boy from his parents. Jesus, you got a God complex or something. You're into taking kids away, aren't you?"

"Calm down."

"Sure, I'll fuckin' calm down. Ok."

He grabs the cabinet from beside Che's bed and upturns it, smashing it onto the floor. Claire flinches. The nurse lets out a little scream.

"Sir, stop it immediately. Security are on their way."

He moves towards her. Claire stares at him, standing her ground, not scared at all. Men like this are cowards. At the last minute he veers away from her and grabs Patch by the arm.

"Leave my fuckin' boy alone." He pulls her away from Che.

Claire feels someone push past her. Knockers has both Jayson's arms pinned.

"Mate. Sorry mate. These pricks are trying to steal my kid." Jayson's whining now. Knockers marches him into the corridor and into the hands of the security guard who's just coming through the ward doors.

As he leaves, Jayson's shouting, "You fuckin' cunt of a doctor. Got the mob to protect you. I'll fuckin' sort you out you blonde cunt, when they're not around."

Knockers comes back in and stands at the end of Triumph's bed without a word.

"It's ok kids," Claire says. "He's just –" What the hell to say? "You're safe now. The man will calm him down. He's angry with me, but it's not your fault."

Both kids continue playing their games, as though nothing's happened. She'd rather see them screaming and crying. To be calm like this, decidedly worrying. They're so used to it. It's their normal.

"Thanks," she says to Knockers.

Knockers turns his back on her. The vicious drooling bulldog on his gang patch seems alive as he moves. Certainly one way to tell the world to keep away.

As Claire takes a few deep breaths to calm herself, her hands tingle. She remembers there's a family waiting to hear some results.

"Whoops, I have to go. Thanks again, guys," she says to Patch.

Just after five Sam shows up at her office, and starts pacing and jiggling his car keys. "I'm meeting them at seven," he says. "Just trying to think of something to say that I haven't already tried."

He's dressed up a bit more than usual.

"Sit down, Sam. Breathe."

It comes down to trust. Types of cancer cell, genes and individual response to treatment make oncology a series of judgement calls that require a huge amount of knowledge and experience. You have to trust your doctor.

"If Roimata had cancer, Sam," she says, "I'd come to you." This is why she feels as sure as she can be about backing him to do the best by Rory. Rory. She thinks of those huge brown eyes, and his trust in adults.

Sam smiles at her and leans back in the chair a little.

"They're terrified. They're in survival mode. You're asking them to let us cut out their precious baby's kidney," Claire says.

"Plenty of patients live very well on one kidney," Sam says. "I've offered to set up a meeting with other families who have been through this."

Sam has brought a list of the treatments they are using, the things they have faith in. "Organic food. Vitamins. Creative visualization. That booster thing," he reads out to her. He rolls his eyes.

"Well, they're all cool. They don't clash with the surgery. The booster thing isn't uncomfortable for him is it?"

"No. I had a look at it. He does have to sit still for long periods. And it's expensive, as are the organic foods."

"Well that is definitely their choice, not ours."

"I know."

"Have you told them they can bring any of these people they want to along tonight?"

"Yes. I hope it's the right thing."

"Oh, yes. Most of these healers are perfectly reasonable. They often advocate both treatments. You may find they help you persuade the family."

"Besides, they may realise they'll look really bad if it's all left to them," Sam says.

She ignores his cynicism.

"Let's make a list of things we could offer to do, that might make them feel more comfortable," Claire says. "I'm happy to have someone in theatre with us, someone who keeps right out of the way but observes or prays, or whatever they want. Not Kate or Isa'ako, but their minister or someone? And, I know, let's ask if they want to record their own voices – talking to Rory, urging him on, soothing him, singing, reading to him, whatever they like – and we could play it on loop during the surgery."

"Really – you'd do that?"

"Of course I would. If it makes them feel better. Actually, I've seen evidence that a mother's voice is powerful. It makes sense to me. I'm wondering at the moment whether we shouldn't do this is in all pediatric surgery."

"You're more open-minded than I thought."

"Watch it. Don't tell anybody." Claire laughs. "I still like evidence."

He stands and she hugs him.

"Whatever happens, Sam, I'll support you. If we have to force them, we'll force them."

"Yeah, well it's all about relationship. So I hope I can improve my relationship with them. I still say they're bloody hippies. Well, she is."

"Use that natural charm and you'll be fine." She laughs again. He still looks so anxious. "Look, where are you meeting them? Why don't I come and wait for you outside and I can stand with you when they film you? If you want me to."

"That would be great. It's at their lawyer's office," and he scribbles down an address. "Thanks Claire. I'll see you there."

Claire feels terrible for the Peterus. But there's one glaring thing they can't ignore. These parents are making a decision that will harm their child. Very occasionally, parents are not the best people to decide. Claire has to believe in her job, in her training. Yes, medicine is imperfect. Science is imperfect. But it's the best thing they have.

She rings Yossi to tell him she won't come to the hospital. She's done what they wanted. She visited her father.

"Claire, I don't think he's got long. You should be here," he says.

"I really want to avoid this child being forcibly taken, Yossi. It's much better if we can come to some agreement with the parents."

"Leave Sam to deal with it."

"This is about the living, Yossi. This boy needs protection."

"I can't believe you would let an old man die with strangers. You are better than that Claire."

Yossi hangs up.

The lawyer's office is in an old villa in Jervois Road. When Claire pulls in and parks opposite at about eight o'clock there is a television crew sitting on the old wooden steps of the house. She sits in her car and works on her laptop, hoping the journalist won't notice her. Dark creeps in gradually.

At about nine thirty, she hears a noise and the door of the house opens and a group of people, including Sam and the Peterus, come out. Two of the crew jump up and point a camera and a microphone at Sam. Claire shuts down her laptop, runs across the road. Sam looks grim and exhausted. When he spots her he shakes his head. Suddenly a ray of bright light is directed at him. He blinks and squints.

"How did it go?" the reporter asks.

Claire goes over to Sam and stands beside him.

"We haven't reached a decision," he says. "We were unable to persuade the family to agree to surgery. I can't talk about the case."

"So you think you know better. You're going to force this child to have surgery against his parents' wishes?"

"I hope very much it doesn't come to that," Sam says.

Claire decides to intervene. "There's no plan yet," she says and starts to guide Sam down the steps and away.

Mrs Peteru steps in front of the camera. "They have their beliefs, we have ours," she says.

Beliefs. Is that what it is? Beliefs, faith, trust. Claire knows these things are powerful, whatever else you think of them.

The reporter follows Sam down the steps. "Do you have the legal right to force this on the family?"

"It could come to that. Our first concern is for our patient. Our patient is the child." Claire leads Sam away and walks with him to his car down the road.

"They're just so certain," he says as he climbs in. "We're going to have to make them."

"You tried," she tells him. "It's all you can do."
"See you tomorrow. Thanks so much."
She waves him off. *I'm heading home now,* she texts Yossi. There's no reply.

40

THEY'RE NOT HOME WHEN SHE gets there. She can't believe they're still up at the hospital with Patrick. Around midnight, Claire is in her pyjamas, putting tuna and crackers in her bag ready for lunch tomorrow when she hears the familiar sound of Yossi's car driving into the garage, and then the front door slam. Yossi comes into the kitchen. He opens the fridge and stares into it.

"How is he?" she asks.

"He's dead."

He puts some bread into the toaster. His cruelty stings more than the news itself.

"Where's Roimata?"

"She's gone straight up to bed. She's exhausted."

Claire drags herself upstairs. Roi's already asleep under the duvet, in her clothes. Claire climbs in with her, holds her. Roi just groans and moves over.

"I love you my darling. I love you round the world a million times." She buries her face in her daughter's thick hair. She'll sleep right here. Comfort her daughter.

She wakes aware that her father is dead. She tests out how it feels. *He's dead. You will never see him again.* It doesn't feel real. Roimata still doesn't stir when she gets out of bed.

Her morning list is routine stuff. Excising a poisonous appendix, repairing an intussusception. She takes a deep breath, the bleach smell in theatre invigorating. She has not thought about the fact the nurses have some rubbish commercial radio station on until she hears, *Coming up in the news, major suspect in historical hitchhiker case dies.* She asks a nurse to turn it off.

After surgery, there's a voice message from Debs. *Oh, Claire, darling, I heard about your Dad. I'm so sorry. Mum and Dad send their best wishes. Let me know about the funeral. I'll call you later.*

At four o'clock she checks her phone. Still no call from Yossi. She'll go home. She hopes Roimata's been sleeping all day. But the house is empty. No note. She calls her.

"We're at the hospital, talking to the social worker."

"Ok. Why?"

"She just wants to know about a funeral and everything. Yossi thought we should come and sit with Patrick's body but it's at the coroner's. And we brought cakes and things for the nurses."

"Are you coming home after that?"

"I think so. Shall I put Yossi on?"

"No, it's ok."

"See you soon."

When they come in the door later that evening Rachel is with them, her arm around Roimata. Yossi doesn't look at Claire, murmuring thanks when she feeds them the lasagna she's made. Rachel mentions several times that the body is alone, clearly uncomfortable with that, but too polite to challenge it. Yossi says he feels the same.

"He was assaulted," Claire says. "The Coroner has to examine him. How else would you have it?"

"You should see your father, Claire," Rachel says. "You could talk to him. Tell him how you feel."

How does she feel?

Debs calls in again, too. "Have you decided when to have the funeral?" she asks.

"I don't know that we'll even have one," Claire answers.

"You have to," Debs says.

Everyone keeps on looking at her and making conversational

openings for her to talk about her feelings. She wishes they would go away. She imagines a bath and a detective novel. Her CEO from work rings. It's very nice of her.

>Yossi comes into the bathroom while she cleans her teeth.
>"Can you stay home tomorrow? See the funeral director?"
>She can't even look at him.
>"Someone has to arrange something," he says.
>She knows how cold she seems. It's how she stays sane, and copes. He'll never understand. She covers her face with the hot facecloth, breathing in the steam. She doesn't take it off until Yossi's gone. It's only then she sees Roimata standing in the doorway, glaring at her. She's not sure how much Roimata heard of the conversation.
>"Goodnight darling," she says.
>Roi turns and goes into her room.

41

The next night Yossi serves her grilled chicken salad with pomegranate seeds, one of her favourites, but she eats without tasting. Sips her wine obediently. No doubt perfectly matched. He's put a lot of effort into the meal. She could never be bothered with all that messy de-seeding. He pours her a dessert wine and leads her to the couch. What can she say to him?

Her stomach lurches at the thought of more wine, but he's hovering, so she takes a sip and the suffusing warmth and sweetness of it relax her, too much. Her head spins. She'll go straight to bed in a minute. Sleep in the spare bedroom. By herself. Yossi always keeps crisp cotton sheets on the bed, ready for a guest. All she wants to do is wash her hair and sink into those sheets.

"Claire, I can only imagine what you have been through that makes you like this."

She tries to smile at him.

"I know you're tired. But we need a decision about Patrick's funeral."

"Yossi, not now. I promise to think about it in the morning."

"But we have to do something. You have to."

"We'll cremate him, I suppose. No service or anything. A funeral director can arrange it all. Just you and me and Roimata." She kicks off her shoes and picks them up.

"He was your father. What will it say to Roimata?"

Claire shakes her head sadly. It will say that her mother comes from a hopeless family. Which is the truth. That is Roimata's inheritance. That's what Claire has passed on to her. If they were going to try to soften that blow, they should have stayed in London.

"Claire, I think you will regret this."

Claire puts her feet on the floor and heaves herself up. She drains the rest of the glass.

"Claire, if you found out for sure he was innocent –"

She gets herself a glass of water to take up to bed.

"I'm going to bed. Good night." Not now, Yossi. Not now.

"Claire, Simon Flaxstone might have some evidence –"

"What?"

"Simon Flaxstone, that guy writing a book. Roi and I have been talking to him."

"Jesus, Yossi. Why have you been talking to him? You promised me."

Roimata's door is open. Claire kicks herself for swearing at Yossi. Roimata will have heard. But why can't they respect her desire for privacy?

Roimata is putting clothes into her backpack. She's crying.

"What are you doing?" Claire asks.

Roimata sobs and keeps folding clothes and stuffing them into the black pack.

"Darling, I'm so sorry. It'll all be over soon."

"Over – when you get rid of your Dad, you mean. When you can just forget all about him. You make me sick."

Claire hears a knock on the door and voices in the hallway.

"Who's that? Is that Brent?"

"Yes, he said I could stay with him and Rachel."

"What?"

"I called him."

"But we hardly know him."

"He's my father," Roimata yells and runs out of the room, slinging the pack over her shoulder.

Claire hurries behind her down the staircase.

"Roimata."

"You can't stop me," Roimata shouts.

Claire sinks to the step she is on, tries to summon her composure. Brent and Yossi are in the hallway looking up at her and Roi is hiding behind Brent. Brent holds up his hands as if to say, *Whoa! Leave me out of this*. Even amongst all this, she notices how much he looks like Roi.

Claire stands up.

"I'm sorry but she needs to stay here," she says to Brent.

"I'm going with him. We're going to be with Granddad," Roimata yells.

What?

"I'm sorry, Claire." Brent is almost backing out of the door. "I told Roi, Māori don't like leaving a body alone. She asked me to sit with Patrick for a while. He's at the funeral home now. I didn't realise you didn't know. Roi, you need to talk to your Mum."

"Roi –" Claire can hardly recognise her own voice.

"You could come too, Mum," Roi says.

Claire feels panicked.

"I don't want to see him." Certainly not with other people there, anyway. But Roimata, this poor girl, caught up in all this horribleness. It's not her fault.

Claire turns to Yossi, who has said nothing. He shrugs.

"Claire, you don't want anything to do with it. Roimata cares."

Yossi is just going to let him take her?

"He's staying at Rachel's. Roi will be fine there."

Brent puts an arm around Roimata. Claire moves over and touches Roi on the arm.

"I'm sorry, Roimata. You go with Brent, have some time out. We'll talk."

"Yes, I am going Mum, whether you like it or not." Roimata opens the door. "And I'm going to sit with Granddad. And we're arranging a funeral. Deal with it." She walks out.

Brent shrugs, his palms up, apologetic.

"I'll bring her back safely. She just needs time out." He follows Roimata.

"Claire," says Yossi. "She'll be fine. She's fifteen."

Claire goes to the spare room and cries and cries and cries. Gentle rain drums on her window. She remembers her father telling her that when he was in prison he had licked the glass to try to get at the rain.

42

Claire's phone buzzes in her pocket during rounds. She glances at it as furtively as she can. Rachel Rakena. She presses Reject.

She must focus at the moment. There's a neuroblastoma to deal with. The baby boy has velvety skin. Mum is Somali and wears a beautiful cornflower blue headscarf. Claire wonders what they have already been through to get here. Now this. It's unbearable. Thank goodness she can give them a hopeful prognosis, the tumour not too advanced. And Sam and Janet are protecting her, doing the work with the family.

Later, in the staff toilets, she listens to her voice messages. Rachel sounds appalled. As she should. *Claire. Roi is quite safe with us. Please let me know if there is anything I can do.*

There's also a message from Brent. *Claire I'm sorry. I didn't know you hadn't agreed to her coming. It's just – well, she said she'd run away if I didn't take her. I thought that was worse. Can we meet up?*

Nothing from Yossi.

When she drives into the carpark near the Rose Gardens, Brent's standing waiting, his khaki shorts perfectly ironed, a white t-shirt displaying strong brown arms. She eases her car into a place. He climbs into the passenger seat, his shoulders almost touching hers, his legs cramped into the small space.

"I love it here," he says, "the view."

The islands rise from the resting sea, unreadable shapes keeping sentinel. It doesn't matter where you go in Auckland, there's always perfectly symmetrical, cone-shaped Rangitoto Island.

"Rangitoto means 'bloody sky'. Must be after some battle,

I suppose," Brent says. "I'm a bit sweaty, sorry. I walked here from Parnell. Enjoying this gorgeous weather. Have you taken Yossi and Roimata to Rangitoto?"

"No."

"I studied it at uni," he says. "I was an expert on lava tubes. Do you know what they are?"

She shakes her head.

"They're formed when lava flows cool on the outside and form a hard crust. Inside, the molten lava flows through them."

"Roimata –" she starts to say, but he speaks at the same time.

"Claire, I'm so –"

Both stop for the other. Claire doesn't know what to say. He beams at her, laughing eyes, confident toss of the head.

"Is it alright if I keep her a few days longer? I don't want to undermine you."

She says nothing, looks out to the water. He tries again.

"I'm going to the Earthsong Music Festival after the funeral tomorrow. It's near Ngāruawāhia. Rachel and I are driving down together. Roi's asked to come too. We'll camp. There'll be heaps of good bands. Look, I'd love to take her with me but Rachel said to check with you first."

"I don't think so. She's fifteen. She can't just run off like she did last night," Claire says.

"Claire, I'll look after her. I promise."

"No."

"She said you wouldn't let her. Ok then, I'll bring her home to you tomorrow night before I head off to the Festival."

Claire doesn't say a word. She wants him to go.

"You'll sort it, Claire. She's just being a teenager."

He climbs out and she watches him walk down the road. Effortlessly cool. She probably should have offered him a lift.

That night she stays late at the hospital monitoring the neuroblastoma baby. She knows she doesn't really need to be right there. She catches up on paper work, the hospital a separate, hushed world.

Yossi texts her. *Roi wants to go to music festival with Brent and Rachel tomorrow. I think a good idea. Get her away from all this. But said I'd check with you first.*

She replies. *No. She's not to go.*

Yossi's left a note on the table.

Hi C, I've gone to bed, sorry. Really tired. Roimata still with Brent. I have arranged for cremation for Patrick at 2pm tomorrow, Purewa Crematorium. There'll be a simple little service first. Have invited a few people. xxxY

Two Māori and a Jew and they end up cremating. Ha. Patrick would have enjoyed that irony. Claire goes to the spare bed, worried sick about Roimata. How can she best get her through all this? Jump on a plane for London is what she'd like to do. Her legs ache and she can't get comfortable. She needs to talk to Roimata. She wonders who will be at the cremation.

What could she tell Roi that might help her understand? She thinks about the day her parents had come to watch her at netball when she was at high school. They'd been living apart but getting on quite well. The first game had gone well. She'd heard Mum ring her father before they left. *Are you sure you're sober?* And he had been sober. Right through the first game. He'd cheered her on. *Go Claire. Jump Claire.*

By the time they started their second game he was gone, only to stagger back halfway through, talking very loudly in his poshest voice and putting his arm around her teacher. Claire remembers trying to concentrate on the game, but getting called for stepping after a crucial intercept. She'd always hated getting things wrong. And then, he was yelling across the court, arguing with the referee so loudly that play had stopped. Sipping from a Coke bottle of clear liquid. Swearing and slurring his words.

But, looking back now, that wasn't so bad. It was her Mum. Claire remembers the weird smile on her face. Claire has always hated that smile. Suddenly she knows why. Her mother had been enjoying it. *See what I have to put up with?* she'd said to the crowd of mums.

She has to get through this for Roimata. She has to be there for Roimata.

43

It's great to get to work early the next morning. Workmen are drilling in the atrium. She has to cram into the lift with two children in wheelchairs. They're teasing each other and laughing. The busyness up on the ward immediately distracts her from the raw ache in her chest. She's in control here, in charge. There are medical students observing her rounds and she talks to them about the way to question children. Knowing what to expect from the child is hard. It's all about developmental awareness, she tells them. Each child is different.

At about ten o'clock a morbidly obese thirteen-year-old is admitted with a broken jaw and some missing teeth. She has a tongue-piercing, which will make it all a bit tricky. The boy who brought her in says she fell off her bike, but the doctor who admitted her downstairs in Emergency thinks she has been punched. So does Janet. The girl won't look at Claire, keeps her eyes cast down. Where are her bloody parents?

"This will take all day. Leave it to someone else," says Janet. "There are plenty of people. You need to go soon."

Claire e-mails her colleague, who will wire the girl's jaw together. The loud 'sent mail' whoosh makes her jump. She doesn't want to leave. This case could be her excuse for not going. She takes a deep breath, afraid of being swept into the vortex that always surrounds her father. Surrounded. Past tense now, he's dead. Don't disappoint Roimata, she tells herself. Whatever you do, do the strong thing. Be wiser. Be kinder.

Should she go home to change? No, her black shorts and cream silky shirt will do. If she goes home, she might just not make it.

She'll drive straight there now.

Claire can't bear the thought of chit-chat so she parks on the street and watches from her car as funeral traffic enters the driveway of the crematorium. Debs and her parents go in. Joe looks different in a suit, and his wife is walking with a stick.

Right on two o'clock she walks down the long driveway in the sun and into the cool of the small chapel. The closed coffin rests on a metal trolley in front of a tall window at the far end. A sandblasted white cross hovers in the centre of the window, floating over the sunlit trees outside. Tall dark curtains frame the view. Waxy gardenias cover the coffin, flawless and beautiful. She's surprised at the jolt of joy the beautiful, peaceful scene and the flowers give her. Jewish families don't even have flowers at funerals, she remembers. Has Yossi done this for her? Or maybe Roimata asked for the flowers?

As her eyes adjust to the dimness, she can see that Yossi, Roimata, Brent and Rachel are sitting in the front. Beside them, a group of three women she doesn't know, shabbily dressed. Behind them sit Debs and her parents. Back further, a couple of men.

Roimata leans against Brent, they whisper and he strokes her hair. Rachel sees Claire and stands, as if to come and get her. Quickly Claire moves to the front and takes the empty chair next to Yossi. He smiles at her, eyes full of sympathy. She knows she should feel something. He whispers to her, "It's time to start. Did you want to speak?" She shakes her head.

A petite woman goes to the front and introduces herself as Jill, the funeral director. She has such a warm manner. She wants them to come up to the front and stand in a semi-circle around the coffin. Claire has no choice but to join in. Yossi holds her hand. It does feel better standing like that.

"Anyone who would like to say something is welcome," Jill says. "First we will hear from Patrick's son-in-law, Yossi."

She nods and smiles at Yossi, who says a few words, about Patrick, about when he was born, his love of music. Yossi seems very uncomfortable, pulling at his suit jacket and shuffling his feet, and his Israeli accent sounds strange here. Claire feels distant, dissociated, as though she is watching all this in a movie.

"Thanks Yossi," says Jill and then nods her head at a woman who looks fiftyish. "Essie has asked to speak. She works at the house where Patrick was living."

Essie puts her hand on the coffin, bowing her head for a minute. Claire can't believe he's in there. She'll never see him again.

"Talofa lava. Hello," says Essie. "Patrick was one of my favourites at the house." She wears black and has a red hibiscus flower tucked behind one ear. "He was a real gentleman. He played music to me. He talked a lot about books, and history. He knew so much. He was always polite. We will miss you at the house, Patrick. We'll miss your jokes. We were so shocked when we heard. Rest in peace."

Essie wipes her head with a hanky. Claire remembers her father's baggy skin, his habit of breathing heavily through his nose. Rachel sings a song in Māori that Claire doesn't recognise. Brent joins in after a while. As Rachel and Brent finish their song they both place a hand on the coffin and bow their heads and Roi quickly does the same. She met him, Claire remembers. Patrick met her beautiful daughter.

As Jill and Yossi roll the coffin away, quiet piano chords are abruptly overwhelmed by plaintive cello. Massenet's Élégie. It's perfect. She and Yossi have listened to it often. He's so thoughtful, Yossi. She's not sure whether her father got to know this piece or not but he would have loved it. All the achiness of life, as the cello can do so well. She thinks of his organs, about to be burned. His bones will survive the fierce heat, so they will be ground to dust. Why can she still feel nothing? Dad. She'll never see him again.

Yossi comes over to her and puts his arm around her. She loves him so much. The room is shimmering. She fears she might faint. She digs her fingernails into the palm of her hand and the sharp pain helps her focus.

"Thank you for organising this," she says, her voice sounding weirdly formal. "I'm sorry you had to do it."

The women from the boarding house come up. Claire wants to run away, but she puts her hand on Essie's arm instead.

"Thank you all for caring for my father." She swallows.

"He was a lovely man," one of the women says.

"He was very proud of you." Essie hugs Claire, almost whispering. "He told us all about your work. You should visit us at the home." They smile at her as they leave.

Claire walks over to Roimata.

"Mum, I'm so glad you came," Roi says.

She has tucked a gardenia behind her ear and she hands one to Claire. Claire hugs her.

"Thank you for all you have done, darling."

Roi smiles and goes back to Brent.

Next, two men approach her.

"Claire, you won't remember me. I'm Detective Sergeant Heenan. I'm investigating your father's death and this is –"

She doesn't hear the rest. Yossi is there beside her now and he reaches out and shakes their hands. Claire closes her eyes. Questions. Always questions. Perhaps about forty interrogations between age four and twelve, when she'd refused to be interviewed any more. It was always cold at the police station. It always seemed to be winter when they talked to her. Some had been kind. One always stank of cigarettes. He'd asked her about her mother's night visitors, her father's drinking, overheard conversations. About the woman at Dad's work who had left her job in the week of the murder. Moira. She'd never even met Moira. About arguments, about money, about whether she could hear her parents having sex in the years her father was home and how often she thought it happened.

But they had never ever made her cry. Not once had she cried in front of them. Her mother cried enough for both of them.

The men and Yossi are looking at her, as though waiting for her to speak. One of them has asked her something. She leans her face in close to his and looks straight into his eyes.

"Fucking leave me alone," she says in a low tone, so Roimata will not hear.

The others are going to go for a drink, but Claire really does have to get to work. She walks slowly down the long driveway bordered by neat gardens, pulling herself together, holding the pure white gardenia up to her face and breathing in the heady scent, breathing it in so deeply she almost forgets to breathe out.

44

YOSSI

AFTER THE FUNERAL, ARIE SUGGESTS a weekend at Waiheke. Just the two of them, drinking wine, listening to music and talking. *No, no, I can't*, is Yossi's first thought. But then, why shouldn't he? Roimata's staying with Brent, and Claire, well, she just seems to do what suits her lately. She'll probably work all weekend anyway, to avoid him. He's glad she came to the cremation, but couldn't she just have told him she was coming? All that trying to explain her behaviour to Roimata, for nothing. And she was so rude to the policemen. Unbelievably rude. Totally unnecessary. What's happened to his strong Claire who can stand up to anything, protect others, who always knows what to do? He's over all the drama that seems to come with Claire here in New Zealand. Getting away will be great.

And it is. When he gets there he flops onto a chair on the deck. Sadness envelops him but the wheel and shriek and splash of the gulls is comforting. He calls Claire to let her know where he is.

"Your father's ashes are at the funeral home. You may want to pick them up," he tells her.

"Why would I do that?"

"Well, I'm not going to. Unless you want him to sit on a shelf forever or be thrown in the bin, you will have to do it."

45

It's strange getting home to an empty house, but a relief as well. She's been rushed off her feet since the service. When the phone rings she takes a deep breath. He has never been so cold to her before.

"Mum, it's me."

"Hi, I thought it was going to be Yossi. He's gone to Waiheke."

"Mum, *please* can I go to the Earthsong Festival? Some friends from school are going. Rachel and Brent will look after me."

"No Roi. You can't just run off like you did. We've got a lot to sort out. Another time."

"You only care about yourself. You don't care about me."

Roimata hangs up on her.

She pours herself another glass of wine and reads the Medical Journal. She puts on Shostakovich, the Piano Trio no 2, which her father had loved.

Dad, he's dead.

She's trying to read about laparoscopic techniques when there's a text from Brent Te Hira. *Bringing her home now.* She puts lipstick on and changes from her dirty jeans into a dress. She wipes the benches, loads the dishwasher, and plumps the cushions. When she answers the door, he hands her a bottle of wine and says he knew it was a rough day for her and he is sorry. He's gorgeous, still. Long, curly hair, rich brown skin and that sensual deep voice.

"I can't believe you won't let me go to the festival," Roimata says. "Aunty Rachel will be there. I'm not a baby."

"No, Roi. You don't just stalk off like that. We need to talk."

Roi stamps upstairs.

"You were wonderful at the funeral," Claire calls after her.

"Like you care!" and Roi slams her door.

Claire is left standing in the hallway with Brent.

"She's mad with me too," he says. "Told me I'm pathetic for not standing up to you. Everything's simple at her age."

"God, let's have a drink," Claire says.

They sit opposite each other.

"She's an amazing young woman. So composed and together," he says.

"I know. She's so calm. I worry about it sometimes."

"I don't think it's a problem. My daughters are too, my other daughters. The kids of this generation are real extremes. Those doing well seem to be amazing. Those not coping are train wrecks."

They talk for a while about his trip to New Zealand, how he finds it, how it's changed while they've both been away.

"Everyone expects you to be the same person you were at twenty when you left," he says.

They've drunk a bit of wine now. She mustn't get to like this man too much. He's not on the birth certificate and she's determined to keep it that way. He might think he has some claim on Roi. She wants to know whether he's thought about it, what he's thinking. But he seems so easygoing, so live-in-the-moment.

"I've been thinking a lot about you today," he says. "I've been trying to think about what it must have been like growing up. I mean, I don't remember the case, but it must have been so weird."

He's on the sofa next to her armchair. It's cosy and their legs are almost touching. He has a habit of looking straight into her eyes. He's so comfortable with himself and with eye contact. She feels flustered, like a young girl.

She wants him to kiss her. She can't even remember what he's said. She laughs and looks down when he looks long into her eyes. He leans over and puts his arm around her. She's not sure whether he's going to kiss her or just comfort her. She puts her mouth up to be kissed but he touches her hair instead and takes her hand.

She starts to cry. She leans into him. He hugs her and his firm grasp makes her bones feel delicate and melty. This is wrong. I need to go to Roimata, she tells herself. She aches to reach out and touch his neck. Every bit of her wants to give herself up to this. You are strong, she tells herself. She stands and gets some tissues from the sideboard, then sits back down beside him.

"You should go," she says.

He tries to kiss her now, moans.

She jumps up and goes to the kitchen, runs water into glasses. She should let Roi go. Poor girl. She'll be safe with Rachel there.

"Are you ok to drive? All that way?" she asks as she hands Brent his water.

"Fine. I'll go home and have a coffee and pack."

"Actually, wait Brent," she says. "I've changed my mind. She can go to the festival. I'll go and tell her."

She runs upstairs to tell Roimata, feeling a lightness and relief. It will be ok. Rachel will be there. Rachel seems solid. She can do this.

She knocks on Roimata's door and goes in. Her window is wide open. There's a note on the bed.

Gone to Earthsong festival.

She hears herself call out the window for Roimata. She peers into the garden. It's still light, but the trees next door cast long shadows. Why hadn't she gone straight upstairs instead of flirting with Brent? She races downstairs.

"Shit, Roi's gone."

She calls Roi's phone. No answer. She calls Yossi and can hardly talk so she hands the phone to Brent who explains, but his voice sounds as though it comes from a radio next door or something.

Then she's back up in the bedroom checking again for her daughter and the room smells of Roimata and violin rosin. She runs down again to Brent.

"Claire, Yossi's ringing Debs to come to you. She'll look on her way over. I'm going looking now. She'll be fine. Kids do this all the time."

She picks up her keys. "I'll start at Great South. You do Market Road," she says.

"Claire. No," he says. "You stay here. She might come back." He goes, running out the door.

She can't find her phone. She had it a minute ago. She rifles through her handbag. Nowhere. Searches the table, the couch. Runs up to the study, tripping on the stairs. She needs to calm down. Back down the stairs. Tips her handbag out onto the couch. There it is, in her bag all the time. She presses on the button over and over. It needs charging. Fumbling as she plugs it in. Needs to stop and think, willing her hands to do what they need to do. They won't seem to quite obey her. And then it hits her. The fact is, she's been drinking. She's upset. She shouldn't drive.

The landline rings and she jumps. Snatches it off the cradle.

"Claire, the ferry's in forty-five minutes. I'll be there in a couple of hours."

She'd hoped it was Roimata.

"Her friends," says Claire. "Who shall I ring? Do we have their numbers?"

"Well she's so new at the school. She's not with Charlotte. I've rung Leilani. She's putting it on Facebook and Twitter. She's texting everyone. She'll find out who has gone, and who Roimata might be with."

The next call is from Rachel. Brent's looked all over and has now decided to drive all the way down to Earthsong. Debs is looking for her around Epsom. Rachel's told the festival organisers, and people will be looking out for her. She's also told the police who can't start a formal search, but have told their officers to keep a lookout. Claire's head spins.

They'll find her. She has to pull herself together. God, she's being pathetic.

She can't stay here and do nothing.

It's out of her control. She's not helping. She rings the police herself.

Debs is there. *I ran away several times when I was a teenager. It's fine, Claire. She will be fine.* Debs tries to comfort her. Makes her cups of tea. Offers her food. Claire doesn't want any of it. Claire sends Roi texts, begging her to let them know she is ok. She rings and all she can get is the answerphone message in the London accent. *Roimata here. Leave me a message. Laters.*

After a while Debs says, "She won't read them if you send too many. You'll drive her crazy."

Yossi arrives from Waiheke, and it's overwhelming to see him. "Go," she says to him, "go and find her."

He tries to hug her but between them is a heavy wall of blame. She has no idea of the time. He looks scruffy and thin and afraid. Find her, Yossi. Find her. Please.

A whole night of pacing and feeling sick. She now knows what people mean by a 'lead weight' in the stomach. No, this can't be happening. Many times she goes to get her car keys, but she has no idea where to look. Rachel rings a few times with comforting words. Tells Claire she has been a great mother, insists that Roimata is a lovely sensible girl and she will be fine. Each time, Claire snatches at the phone. But each time there is no news.

Debs falls asleep on the sofa. Claire opens the door for fresh air. It's still warm. There are a few stars. She goes out into the garden. Above her, the window is open where Roimata climbed out and down the trellis.

I'll do anything, she tells the darkness. Anything. Just keep her safe.

It is the closest she has ever come to praying.

46

When her mobile rings at six in the morning, it wakes her. She must have fallen asleep in the armchair. As though a fist has punched into her stomach she remembers about Roi. She leaps on her phone. The screen says it's her CEO from the hospital. What? How does she know about Roi?

"They've found him, Claire."

Him?

"Rory Peteru. The police found the family. We have him here, we're prepping him. He hasn't eaten since seven last night. Can you operate in an hour? Best we just get it done before it can all be debated again. They'll injunct us as soon as they can."

What? She stretches. "Ok. Yes, I can do it. I'll be there," she says.

Debs wakes and tries to dissuade her but she needs to do this.

"It'll distract me," she says.

Debs even rings Yossi, but he tells her to let Claire do it.

"He said, Claire is Claire, this is what she does. Tell her we will find Roimata," Deb tells her.

Trust me Claire, he texts, *I am her father.*

At the hospital gate, there's chaos. Reporters, cameras. She holds her head very still, stares straight ahead and drives through the gates and into the gloom of the basement, parks and sits for a second. Can she do this? It's important not to operate if she's too upset, but she knows she can.

She feels tiny against the huge doors that separate the theatre area. They bear the legend AUTHORISED PERSONNEL ONLY.

She turns her back and shoves with her backside to open them.

Focus. Forget. Observe. As she cuts and lifts out Rory's kidney, she can see the tumour. She deals with it. Clinically. Cleanly. There's every chance this child will lead a normal life. What he does with his life is not down to her, thank goodness.

Kate and Isa'ako Peteru are waiting in a meeting room near PICU. Claire looks through the grubby glass for a minute. She doesn't have to talk to them. Sam could do it all, the CEO's involved, and their clinical leader is here too. But she'd pushed hard for this. And it was her hands inside Rory. It was her belief that led to this.

Kate looks up, her face streaked and crumpled, her long limbs folded in on themselves.

"The surgery went well," Claire lets them know. "We'll watch him closely but the surgery went absolutely to plan, no problems at all."

Kate turns away and buries her head in Isa'ako's chest. His eyes are closed and his lips move as though he's praying. Claire sits down. She wants to touch Kate, put her hand on her knee or something.

"What, do you want me to thank you?" Kate says.

"I'm truly sorry you have been through so much. He should be well now. He really should. We just have to watch how he recovers. But problems at this stage are rare."

Isa'ako reaches past his wife and pats her shoulder.

On her way out through the public waiting room a Samoan woman, perhaps Isa'ako's mother or aunt, rushes up, weeping, and envelops Claire in a huge hug.

"Doctor, Doctor, thank you so much. God has answered our prayers. God sent you to help us."

Leaving the hospital is a blur. Somebody wants to talk to her, some people give their congratulations. Their voices come to her from a different world, miles away.

In her car, she rings Brent, who answers instantly.

"Hi Claire."

She can tell from his voice there is no news. She can't speak.

"Nothing. I am so sorry. I am sure she will be fine."

"Thank you." She's not sure whether she says it out loud or not. She hangs up. Looks at her phone.

She calls Roimata. That answer phone again. *Laters.*

Please come home safely.

The funeral parlour is in a modern brick building in Remuera Road. It's a bit tired. Plenty of parking though. There's a sign on the door. *Please Come In.* The receptionist with big hair that must have suited her ten years ago interrupts her phone-call and, holding the receiver to her chest, asks Claire how she can help. She goes through a door behind her and comes back with a midnight blue box made of thick cardboard. The colour has been carefully chosen. Tasteful. Sombre, but not funereal. Placing it on the desk in front of her she checks the label. CREMATED REMAINS OF: Bowerman, Patrick James.

"Is that correct?"

As the woman hands it over, still holding the phone, another line ringing, she pushes a form at Claire and motions her to sign it. Claire signs without reading.

"Have a good day," the woman says as she leaves.

The box is strangely light. Before she drives off she makes sure no-one is looking and then kisses it gingerly. "Dad. I love you," she tells the box, then puts it on the seat beside her.

On the way back she takes a detour into Parnell.

There's a flat she used to live in at the bottom of a street that runs down to the water. She glances at it as she drives past. The rundown two-storied house in four flats has been renovated and turned back into a gracious mansion.

Hobson Bay laps at the bottom of the road. There are new houses crowded down there and cars parked along both sides of the road. It's all neat and tidy with planted bush and a walkway. At the bottom she pulls over and peers through to the estuary. Here would be one place she could scatter Patrick.

She looks at her phone again. Texts Roimata.

Roi, I have picked up Granddad's ashes. Let us know you are ok.

Signs warn that workmen are removing the huge concrete sewer pipe that used to cross the bay and replacing it with underwater ones. But it's deserted today. Claire had loved walking out across the old pipe. It had been safe, about five feet wide, but it had felt as though you were walking on water and from halfway across you could see across Tāmaki Drive out to the sea.

She climbs out of her car. A kingfisher trills cheerfully. She looks up at a lamppost and there's the bird, vivid blue and green. She walks down the path. It smells muddy and rotten eggy. Hydrogen sulphur.

Looking up the road she can just see the highest window of her old bedroom imprisoned behind its new fence. She'd found her father a flat nearby in Gladstone Road. A basement flat. She'd thought if she could show him some love, listen to music with him, make him laugh, he might be happy. She'd tried so many times. Put dressings on his cuts and scratches, sorted his benefit, tipped out his alcohol, listened to his slurred promises. Only to be called by police to come and pick him up from A and E, or the side of the road, or the Rose Gardens, in a drunken stupor. Always, the urine and the vomit. And always, the flirting with her flatmates, her friends, her neighbours.

She walks back to her car and lifts out the blue box, heads around the barrier and along the muddy foreshore. She says to the box, "You're keen to go. You've had enough, right?"

She stops still, hushed. Five metres in front of her, on the mudflats, a heron clenches a dead tree branch in its powerful claws – upright, curved neck, small snake-like white head.

It's almost over. She stares at the box, awkward to carry. It's not her father. He's gone.

Her phone rings. The heron swoops away with a flutter of feathers. It's Roi's number.

"Roi, darling?"

A whimper.

"Roi? Are you ok?"

A sob.

"Are you ok?"

"Yes."

"Oh God darling." She starts to cry. "I'm so sorry."

"I'm sorry too Mum."

"Have you found Yossi?"

"Yep, he's here. I'm sorry Mum."

"That's ok. It's great to hear your voice."

"Here's Dad."

"Claire? She's fine, she's good."

She cries out, her whole body slumps.

"Claire, are you ok?"

"How did you find her?"

"She texted me. She's been fine. Some uni students picked her up. They seem very nice, she's been sharing their tent."

"God."

"I know. We can't think about what could have happened. We'll leave as soon as we can."

Claire looks down at the blue box under her arm, brings it up to her face and brushes her cheek against its cold lid.

They found her, Dad.

They found her.

She continues down the path, the mud getting thicker and wetter. She stops and opens the box. A waxy plastic bag folded and stapled.

The mangroves suck in air, snorkel-like with their tentacle roots. They squelch and pop. She remembers from a school science class that they don't have seeds like other plants. They grow their babies on them somehow, protecting them until they drop. They can float, these baby mangroves, and have an emergency food supply onboard to last them until they find the right soil.

Roimata is alive.

But Patrick is dead. She puts the lid on the box and heads back up the path. It's not the right time to scatter him yet. She needs to talk to Roimata and Yossi about him. Gulls screech and wheel.

They get home after dark. Claire hears the car, goes rushing out and almost drags Roimata out of the car to hug her. She desperately wants to snuggle in to her, kiss her all over like she did when Roi was a baby, but she knows she can't. She wills herself to act low-key and calm. *She is a separate person*, she remembers Deb saying to her, *she is not you.*

Roi's a bit sulky, a bit embarrassed. Doesn't say much. Goes straight up to bed.

When Claire looks in on her, Roi is pretending to be asleep. Claire leans over and kisses her.

"Mum. I'm sorry," Roimata says, keeping her eyes closed.

Claire sits down on the bed. She'd like to tell Roi never to hitchhike again, but this is not the moment.

"Tell me about that reporter?"

"He's great. He says Granddad is innocent."

"Does he have evidence?"

"He was writing this book on gangs. This guy, from the Mongrel Gang, or something like that, told him one of them had murdered that girl."

"That's not evidence. He could be lying. Boasting. If there's any new evidence – like forensics or something – then I'll want to know."

"He says your Dad was there, but the gang took the girl away from him."

"My Dad was there?"

"He was with the girl out in the country, and the gang came and threatened him and took the girl off him."

"According to Simon."

"He said he's got loads of proof."

"But why wouldn't my dad have just said so? Told someone? Instead of going to prison."

"Simon said he thinks your dad was ashamed. Guilty because he was there and he didn't protect the girl. I think he was drunk."

Claire remembers what Patch had said. That the gang was involved. Why was her father even there? She supposes it will all come out.

"Roi, don't talk to that journalist please. They can twist things. Nothing's off the record."

"But will you talk to him?"

"Yes, I'll listen to what he has to say. When things calm down a bit. Now go to sleep. You must be so tired."

Claire heads to the door.

"Mum, how old were you when the girl disappeared?"

"I was just a baby, darling."

"Babies can't remember," Roimata says, sounding relieved.

Claire's not so sure that's true.

As she lies in the spare bed, longing for sleep, she tries not to think about what might have happened to Roi. She and Yossi have hardly spoken.

She remembers reading to Che MacKenzie just a few days ago. God, he hadn't known what sand and sea were. He's never been to the beach. She can't believe it. He lives in Auckland, and he's never been to the beach.

She fantasises about adopting him. Taking him to London. His slightly sour smell, his unblinking eyes. His quietness. She is growing dangerously fond of this boy. It's getting unprofessional. Of course she can't adopt him. Christ, look at the mess she's making of her own life. Can't save anyone else. She knows what she'd be taking on. How much hurt, how much commitment. She hopes whoever does take him understands that.

She must see if she can get him *Ferdinand the Bull*. She and her father had loved that book. He'd read it over and over to her. Dad. Gone. She thinks about his whiskery kisses.

47

Yossi's friend Arie sails them across to Ruby Bay in his catamaran. Claire wears a wide-brimmed hat and sunglasses. Rachel has a photo of Patrick she's cut out from the paper and she's perched it on the hatch and draped ivy around it. As Yossi carries the ashes on board, Rachel says a prayer in Māori.

"We can see the Coromandel today. Wasn't your Dad born there, Claire?" Rachel says.

"Yes, Thames. His family were gold miners."

They tie up against the jetty at Ruby Bay and then troop into the bush. Rachel tells Roimata the names of all the plants.

When they stop there's a burst of birdsong.

"That a bellbird?" whispers Brent.

"Yeah," says Rachel.

"Wow," says Yossi, when it's finished. "I read about them releasing bellbirds on the Island just recently. What do they look like?"

"They're tiny," Rachel says.

Yossi tries to hand the blue box to Claire but she motions at Roimata.

"Roi?" Yossi says.

She takes the ashes and starts pouring.

Haere, haere, haere. Rachel begins to farewell Patrick.

Yossi follows, speaking Hebrew in a low voice and then translates. *As for man, his days are like grass; as the flower of the field, so he flourishes. For the wind passes over it, and it is gone.*

Claire puts her cardy around her shoulders.

It won't take long.

They're paler than she expected. They look like sand. It's almost over.

Dad. Goodbye Dad. I'm sorry you had such a horrible life. I'm sorry I didn't do more to help you.

Rachel starts to sing softly. Brent joins in. Claire knows they're not that comfortable with scattering ashes, but they're there for Roi. And her. Yossi comes to stand beside Roi and puts his arm around her. The song swells and then it's over.

Goodbye Dad.

There's something she'd really like to do. But it breaks all the rules. She can't do it on her own, she'd chicken out. "Yossi," she says when they are nearly in Auckland. "I'd like your help tomorrow. There's this child at work, Che, I told you about. He's leaving the hospital."

48

As they step out of the lift to the foyer on their way out of the hospital, a familiar black T-shirt comes towards Claire. Jayson has his arm slung around Heaven's neck and he almost drags her along.

Heaven notices them first, stops walking, mouth open, then stumbles as Jayson drags her by the head into the lift.

"Jayse, Jayse," says a startled Heaven.

Jayson's ignoring her, but then he sees them.

"What the fuck?" he yells.

The lift doors are closing. He puts his hand in the way and slowly the doors open and he drags Heaven out again.

Claire and Patch walk faster. Patch picks Che up and holds him to her. He just snuggles in, looking at the ground. She's awkward now, one arm holding Che, the other reaching for Triumph but also holding a chunky carseat. Claire gathers up Triumph and they're both running.

"Hey, you cunt, where you taking that kid?"

Jayson is right behind them. Claire gets herself between Jayson and Patch. She feels his hand on her shoulder as she reaches the front door.

"Put that kid down you gang ho. Don't touch my kid with your dirty mongrel hands!"

An old man stops and stares, and a young Mum grabs her two children by the hand and runs out of the door and away down the path.

From the front entrance appears Feleti, gentle giant security guard. He's dealt with Jayson before. Claire knows him well, has often chatted to him on her way in and out of the hospital.

"Sir, come with me."

"She's got the fucking kid."

Feleti gets Jayson in an arm lock. Claire smiles at Feleti over her shoulder as she and Patch run to her Audi which waits opposite in the P2 drop-off zone. Get-away driver Yossi drives off, sedately, not like in a movie.

"Yippee ki-yay," he yells.

Che chuckles.

Shit, now it's probably abduction.

"Yahoo! Yossi, this is Patch, Che, and –" she turns towards the back seat and, in a posh voice, holding her hand palm up to present him, "– Mister – Triumph."

Triumph giggles. Patch is fiddling with her seatbelt, between the two kids.

"Now I'm in the shit. Deep Shit, Arkansas," Claire says softly to Yossi, rolling down her window and feeling the air ruffle up her hair.

As they drive over the bridge Claire laughs, thinking of the paraphernalia she would have schlepped down to Worthing or Brighton, had this been a trip for Roimata at Che's age: sunscreen, hats, togs, towel, drinks, food, book, rug, cushions, water wings, bucket and spade, wet wipes, sunglasses, spare clothes, blankie, Dogga, first aid kit. If Yossi were with them, he'd have added wine and glasses, homemade cupcakes, his iPod and connection to the car stereo, with a special playlist for the occasion.

Instead, just a gang woman, two kids, one in a hospital gown, and an ex-Israeli army getaway driver who drives like a nana. It's fun.

There's a t-shirt of Roi's in the boot so, in the car park, Claire whips off Che's hospital gown and pops the t-shirt on him. It comes down to his knees. STELLA it says in sequins across his little chest.

As soon as they get to the sand, Yossi and Claire kick off their shoes and roll up their jeans. Patch looks around her, with wide eyes. She makes no move to take off her cheap black ankle boots or even her jersey, and the woolly hat stays on her head in spite of the brilliant sunshine.

The kids are agape. Triumph is in Patch's arms and when she tries to put him down he whimpers.

Yossi holds out his good arm and gently takes the wee boy, who looks as though he might cry. Claire helps lift Triumph onto Yossi's shoulders. He sets off down towards the water and the boy's whimper turns to a shout of delight.

Che hasn't made a sound. Claire bends down and takes his worn, too-small sneakers off him. He's not sure, but he lets her. When she goes to put them in a pile with hers, though, he reaches out and picks them up, holding them to his chest. She gets it. He doesn't own much. She lets him hold them for now.

She takes his hand and they walk down towards the water. Yossi runs into the shallows and, when a wave comes, runs out again just ahead of it, giggling and shouting. Triumph, holding on tightly around Yossi's chin, laughs and laughs.

Claire leads Che down to the water and puts her toe in, jumping at the cold. She breathes in deeply, loving the tangy, fishy air. It invigorates her. Che pulls away, not letting her tug him in. She stays right at the edge of the water with him, taking it at his pace, gently encouraging, laughing at the shocked look on his face when he touches the cold water with his toe. But he's not ready to go in. She cajoles, but gently. Even feeling the sand between his toes is something.

Then Yossi comes over, handing Triumph to her.

"Watch this," he says to Che. He kicks water at Claire. Che watches Claire. He looks fearful and alert, expecting anger. Claire laughs, makes a wide 'O' with her mouth, in mock surprise, and then laughs again. She kicks some water back at Yossi. He splashes her again. Then he says to Che, "Splash her."

Claire pretends not to have heard and then squeals when Che kicks a tiny spray of water at her jeans.

Just five minutes later, he is running in and out, sloshing and wading, jumping and landing on two feet, thinking it hilarious when he sprays Claire. Splashing her again and again. Every time she pretends to be surprised. Every time he giggles with delight. Triumph chuckles too and buries his face in her shoulder, her face brushing his coarse sticky-up hair.

An hour and a half just scoots by. Yossi shows Che how to skip stones. Yossi can make his skip three or four times. Che whoops with delight when his skips once.

When he puts his shoes down beside Patch, who sits on the sand shaping the letters C H E, they show him leapfrog. Patch, who must be sweltering in her heavy clothes, does join in the leapfrog. When she goes to jump over Yossi he stands so that he has her piggybacked, holds her with his one good arm, and runs around with her. She's almost crying with laughter. She has a deep belly laugh.

"Careful, Yoss. She's pregnant."

He sets her down gently. "She's tough, this one," he says.

Patch beams.

Yossi and Patch take the kids down to the kiosk at the end of the beach and buy ice-creams. Claire lies in the sand and lets the sun creep through her pores, into her bones.

She sits up and watches them walk along the beach and she admires Yossi, so energetic, so happy, and so wonderful with these kids. There's a longing, deep in her gut.

When they're almost back at the car, Patch says, "I never knew the sea would be so noisy."

As they drive away, Che says, "I saw the seaweed goes pop and squirts out all over Yossi."

Triumph says, "Yothi, pop." And falls asleep.

All we can give children is memories, Claire thinks.

49

ON THE DRIVE HOME, A text from Janet: *Knockers took care of it. Jayson too scared of him. Hasn't even told anyone.*

She reads it to Patch, who laughs with delight.

"Go Knocks," she says.

"Go Knocks!" says Yossi.

Claire laughs.

"Thank you, Yossi." She puts her hand on his sun-warmed leg.

By the time they get to Starship, Heaven and Jayson are long gone. The social workers have notified them that they can't take Che home.

"It was fantastic," she tells Janet, as she hands the two sandy, tired children back into her care. "But bloody unprofessional. Still can't believe I broke so many rules. Am I going to lose my job?"

"I've covered for you," says Janet. "Nobody knows."

After Knockers and Patch have been outside for a smoke, it's time to discharge Triumph. He's doing so well. Claire goes through the paperwork with Patch.

"Knockers says that dude, he couldn't wait to get to some party, eh, and they went off to start drinking. I'd like to smash him," Patch says.

Claire just hopes Knockers didn't sell Jayson drugs. That's the reputation of his gang. She's not going to ask.

Patch gives her a hug.

"We're gonna call this one Bowerman if it's a boy. Star if it's a girl," she tells Claire again.

"You are a wonderful Mum," Claire tells Patch, who blushes.

At four that afternoon she's in PICU when her pager beeps. She goes up to the ward to say goodbye to Che. The foster mother looks a nice enough woman, plump, oily hair, a bit worn down by life, and with two kids of her own. She's left them with a friend, so she can concentrate on Che, which is a good sign.

"Hi Che. I'm Julie. We've got a doggy at our place."

A bit too perky, perhaps, but she's trying. She's brought some chippies and a box of juice. Sipping on the straw, Che goes with her without complaining, which breaks Claire's heart.

"Bye darling." Claire hugs him as they wait for the lift. Help him. Help this little boy.

When she gets to her office, Yossi's there with a huge bunch of flowers. Delphiniums, snapdragons, sunflowers. He beckons her over to the window and they watch the woman and Che walking up a slope, past the adult hospital, then out of sight.

"At least she's holding his hand," Yossi says.

He reaches for her and holds her. She starts to cry, her chest tight with grief and fear.

50

Claire drives to Grey Lynn, to the street where her father was living before he died. This might have been her life had she stayed here in New Zealand. Hundred-year-old wooden villas, renovated to within an inch of their lives. Garages and carports gouged out under foundations, gracious decorative verandahs hoisted into the air to make room for cars.

She stops outside number 30. It's a huge, once gracious house, surrounded by an odd collection of added-on buildings from different eras. At the top of the stairs, there's a laminated piece of paper instructing her to ring a bell. It looks dangerous, the bell press, dangling from wires that are clearly meant to be behind the wall, half-hearted strips of insulation tape hanging off exposed wires.

What is it about her family that they frequent places like this? She's visited them in psychiatric institutions, prisons. Her mother did a stint in a women's refuge once and dragged Claire with her. Worn carpet, rotting wood, plastic flower arrangements, notice boards and fake-cheerful décor. Places for people who didn't cope. Well, she, Claire, was always going to cope. She'd decided that early on.

A cheerful young man leads her to Patrick's unit, which she struggles to open with the key they have given her. She looks down at her feet on the rotting verandah. He walked on here.

She almost drops her handbag while trying to juggle the lock. The door finally gives. There's that smell again. She doesn't know what it is. There's unwashed clothes, of course, an old man smell. There's a hint of instant coffee.

His narrow single bed is on wheels and, as she puts her hand on it, it moves. It's unmade and has a dingy maroon and green cover that someone at some stage must have thought smart. The sheets and pillowcases don't match, but then, whose do?

Against the wall leans a new imitation-cane chair, which stands out among the battered, weary furniture. On the wall, a laminated list of instructions headed *In Case of Fire*. A poster of some obscure painting hangs crookedly. Someone, sometime, presumably thought this would add cheer but the light has faded it and every detail of the painting is now a dirty pink. Her father would have hated it, but clearly had no longer cared enough to take it down.

She wanders into the kitchenette. It's clean and tidy. There's no character, nothing to show who her father was. There's a dish-drainer with a plastic colander, a plate, and a mug still sitting in it. A used tea-bag in a glass, yellow and dry.

Back in the main room, Claire shakes out the rubbish bags she's brought with her. This bag can go to the Sallie Army. She opens the closet and starts pulling out fleecy jackets and worn track-pants. There's a layer of papers and bits and pieces on the floor of the closet.

Funny, the things that undo us. Claire sorts through piles of photos. Baby photos, wedding photos, her mother looking young and happy. What stops her in her tracks, though, knocks the breath out of her, and leaves her standing in the middle of the room gasping like a stupid goldfish, is not a photo but a battered copy of *Winnie the Pooh*. He'd read it so well. They'd laughed so much. They'd always shared this sense of humour; her mother thought them silly and childish. Right through her childhood, when she'd had times of contact, her father would hold her close and call her *a bear with a pleasing manner but a positively startling lack of brain.* They both loved to say, *Time for a little something* – when they were headed into the kitchen to search for snacks.

She sits down on the bed. A man walks past the window of the unit, singing loudly, *I see red, I see red, I see red,* and playing air guitar. She must pull herself together, get on with what she's here to do. She stands and starts to divide the photos into those she supposes she ought to keep but doesn't want to, and those of scenery and people that mean nothing to her. She finds herself holding one photo, staring at it. She can't think. Maybe they should all just go in the bin. Easier.

Her phone beeps. It's a text from Yossi. *Can I come and help? Roi's with Rachel.*

She sits down on the bed. Takes a deep breath. She's not ok. She needs help. She needs Yossi.

Thanks. Yes.

She can carry on now, knowing Yoss is coming. She becomes efficient. She'll keep the photos. She looks at each one before slipping it into a bag.

Yossi taps on the door. He comes in, his eyes wide with sympathy and love. He hugs her for a long time. She weeps.

"My darling."

"I'm ok, honest."

"I know you're ok, but it's bloody hard."

Yossi starts shaking out a rubbish bag.

"It's so hard, not knowing whether he murdered that girl," he says.

"Yossi, you still don't get it."

He hugs her.

"You could try telling me."

"It's not about the murder. It's the whole thing. He drank. I couldn't trust either of them. I've worked hard to get up out of that miserable place they lived in. I just want to be happy. I just want to survive."

"Claire, I am so sorry –"

"I'm sorry too, I've been such hard work since we came back."

"I made you come. Was it so wrong?"

"It's been hard. But then," she looks around, "I guess this is good –" She sees her father's CD collection in a worn cardboard box. "Now this, I want to keep. It's precious."

"I brought my iPod and mini-speaker. Do you want to listen to some music? Or we can talk. Do you want to talk about Patrick?"

"Music would be great."

He puts on The Style Council. Cruisy. Catchy. Perfect.

51

NEW ZEALAND 1970

Your wife is hysterical, both of you exhausted from listening to the baby crying all night. You hear her ring your office, shout ugly things about you, hang up, and weep. The baby screams and screams. A drive in the car might put her to sleep, give your wife a break, get you out of there. How do you end up on a hot side road, abandoning a girl who needs your help?

She stands barefoot in the sticky road looking back at you, in her red dress, her blonde hair tumbling out of its Raquel Welch look, clutching her dress-up shoes to her chest. Behind her comes a dark green Charger, muscled arms spilling out windows, fingers raised. The men shout and swear, calling to her, leering. You've heard of these new gangs. The guys at work want to line them up and shoot them. Seeing them in the flesh, the swastikas tattooed on their arms and faces offend you.

You call out to the girl, desperate, "Quick, come here, and get in the car."

She gives you the fingers and keeps walking towards the Charger, swaying and unsteady but still with her sexy walk. They stop, call to her and while she climbs in they're grinning at you. You climb out to go over, to warn her, but one guy wearing some kind of German war helmet lazily gets out of the Charger, comes and hits you in the face, hard. You look at the girl again and she stabs her two fingers in the air.

You'll go over that moment for the rest of your life. Close your eyes against the glare of the sun thumping in your head as you strain to see. Smell the stench of fertiliser, beer, and your own sweat. Hear the roar of the Charger idling. Turn your head to avoid the ugly hatred of the swastika tattoos. Reach out to catch the girl's stumbling.

Most of all, though, you'll remember the first thin wails of the baby in the carry-cot on the back seat of your car. The way the animal who'd hit you looked toward your Holden. The way you'd almost forgotten the baby was even there.

This is terror now. You have to save your baby, Claire. It's your baby or the girl. The girl will be all right. She's old enough to look after herself.

Get your baby out of this mess. Drive away. No-one must ever know. You can see the 'told you so' victory of your wife's martyrish disappointment in you; you can hear her wails and her spewing hatred. She must never know.

Claire's wide awake most of the way back to Auckland. You stop at the side of the road and put her carrycot on the passenger seat beside you. Every time you look at her she's alert, looking around, jerking her arms and legs. She's soaking up everything like a big sponge. The car stinks of beer and of your hot fear. You don't know how to comfort her, what to say, what to do. You can't calm down: you talk to her, but it sounds desperate. You rock her but, in your panic, too fast. You stroke her, but not gently enough.

It's as though she knows. As though her nerves and her muscles will remember this, though she will never have the language for it.

52

WAIHEKE ISLAND

It's a grey day but the sun shows itself every so often. Twice, while Claire gets dressed, kererū whoosh past at a startling speed. Rachel says they're there to bring luck to the wedding.

"We get them here every day. They love the berries on the pūriri trees," says Claire. "They seem to travel in pairs. They can be real show-offs sometimes, swooping and gliding. I guess it's a mating dance."

They've decided to go for a little drama to start the wedding. Debs has talked Claire into a bit of theatre, a bit of effect. *It's the one time*, Debs keeps telling her. *It's your one chance. Relax, girl, and enjoy it.* And to her own amazement, she does.

Joe has brought his boat down from Russell and at three in the afternoon, he picks up Claire, Debs, and Roimata from the jetty and takes them out a wee way and drops anchor. Joe's kind then, teasing Claire, feeding her a bit of brandy and distracting her by telling stories about the history of Ruby Bay. Roimata keeps hugging her all the time.

"Mum, I love you so much," she says.

Half an hour later, Debs' phone plays a U2 ringtone and she says, "That's the signal. All ready on the shore."

Rachel's voice rings out in a welcoming karanga call from the jetty. Her keening flies around the bay, dying away into the bush, and Claire shivers and tries not to cry. *Haere mai. Haere mai.* They have talked about the words of the karanga and also the way Māori call to the dead to stay with the dead, and the living to stay with the living. *Te hunga mate ki te hunga mate, te hunga ora ki te hunga ora.* Entirely appropriate. Sure, Rachel believes the spirits of the dead are there with them, in the bush, in the sky, in the water. Claire interprets it as telling the past to leave them alone. Put it behind them. Nothing supernatural. She simply does not believe the dead are here with them in any actual way. But they're here in their influence on them all, the way they're shaped, in their genes and their energy and their attitudes. She understands it that way. She thinks of her mother and father.

Haere mai. Haere mai. Joe slowly pilots the boat towards the shore in response to the karanga and Claire can see them all now on the jetty, waiting for her.

"What a motley lot," she says to Debs, who smiles and says, "Your motley lot."

"My motley lot," says Claire. She is holding the bouquet of perfect yellow dahlias Debs presented her with this morning.

"What they have in common is that they love you. They all wish so much good for you and Yossi and Roi, you know."

"I know. Now stop being nice to me. I'm going to get through this whole day without crying."

Joe goes alongside and ties up. Then he takes her hand and whispers in her ear, "You look radiant, my dear. And your parents would be so proud," as he helps her onto the jetty.

Rachel's karanga dies away and the next minute Brent steps forward and begins a haka. Handsome in his dark suit he stamps his feet, eyes rolling and tongue flicking, his face jerking slightly up to the right, slightly up to the left. He places a perfect green leaf on the wooden deck and backs away, still challenging them.

Roi, looking older than usual in her green dress and showing lots of smooth brown skin, reaches down and picks up the leaf, smiles, then steps back in line with Debs. Claire touches Roi's hair and hugs her.

Yossi steps forward, beaming from ear to ear. Tears stream down his face. Claire hugs him to her tight, and her tears flow too. She loves him so much. He is the kindest man in the world. The celebrant leads them through their simple vows, there on the jetty.

Afterwards on the deck, Arie puts klezmer music on the stereo and he and his girlfriend and Yossi put their arms around each other's necks and dance the hora, whirling and laughing, grabbing Sam and Janet, who join in. Rachel and Brent join the circle too, looking as though they've done it all their lives. Yossi pulls Roi to her feet and dances with her as they often do in the kitchen for fun. He looks across to Claire and she can tell he's bursting with pride. He loves her. She believes it.

The sun pushes through the clouds and people's voices get lazier and Claire's skin rises to the warmth through her gauzy sleeves. Before they eat, Rachel stands and speaks, elegant as always in her black dress and long red jacket. A cool, luminous greenstone pendant hangs around her neck and she hangs a similar one around Yossi's neck. She pays tribute to her Nana Roimata, lying under her beloved mountain and Papa Donald, lying next to the beautiful River Arno in Florence.

"I know you hate this spooky stuff," she teases Claire, "but it was Donald who brought you and Brent and Roi together. And it took Yossi, dear Yossi, to bring you all here to us." She talks about Yossi's parents lying in Israel and Claire's parents lying not far away.

Roimata stands and sings with Rachel, showing off her new moves with the poi, not skilled yet but confident, flicking her head and widening her eyes, as green as her dress. She stands straight and holds her head high. Where did this poised young woman come from?

After they've all eaten too much and had too much wine and it's almost time to leave for the ferry, Claire thanks them for coming and says there's one thing she's saved until last. She smiles at Roi, who raises her violin and plays Claire's favourite Bach sonata. Everyone is silent as the exquisite sound joins the sigh of the bush and the slap of the water. Yossi grins at her and Claire thinks her heart will burst. Everyone she loves is here with her, safe and peaceful, at least for this moment.

THE END

GLOSSARY OF MĀORI WORDS AND PHRASES

Ātaahua	Beautiful
Haere mai	Welcome
Haere mai ki te whānau	Welcome to the family
Haka	Ceremonial dance
Hei Tiki	Carved pendant, often made of greenstone
Hongi	To press noses in greeting
Hui	Gathering, meeting
Karanga	Ceremonial call on to the marae
Kaumātua	Elder
Kete	Flax baskets
Kuia	Female elder
Marae	Communal place
Nā mihi	With regards (sign-off for letter)
Pākehā	New Zealander of European descent
Patu	Club-shaped weapon
Poi	A light ball on a string which is swung to music
Taiaha	Spear-shaped ceremonial weapon
Te Reo	The Māori language
Tēnā koe	Greetings (to one person)
Tēnā koutou katoa	Greetings (to all)
Tikanga	Correct protocol
Tūrangawaewae	Place where one belongs through kinship
Urupā	Burial ground, cemetery
Waka huia	Treasure boxes
Whānau	Extended family
Wharenui	Meeting house

ACKNOWLEDGEMENTS

For Ruthie, my dear little sister. (1965-2010)

Special thanks to Dr Dwayne Crombie.

Heartfelt thanks to Anthea Springford, Dame Lesley Max, Hilary Smith, Beni Kay and Ein Harod Kibbutz, Janet French, Wendy Nelson, Boaz Shulruf, Dr Simon Rowley, Stephanie Johnson, James George, Rachael King, Gloria Drury, Gillian Ewart, Geoff Walker, Fiona Copland, June Jelas, Ann Glamuzina, Katie Henderson, Judith White, Scott Younger, and the New Zealand Society of Authors.